Other Books by Janet Tashjian,
Illustrated by Jake Tashjian

Einstein the Class Hamster

The My Life Series:
My Life as a Book
My Life as a Stuntboy
My Life as a Cartoonist

by Janet Tashjian

Fault Line
For What It's Worth
Marty Frye, Private Eye
Multiple Choice
Tru Confessions

The Larry Series:
The Gospel According to Larry
Vote for Larry
Larry and the Meaning of Life

Praise for **My Life as a Book**

★ "Janet Tashjian, known for her young adult novels, offers a novel that's part *Diary of a Wimpy Kid*, part intriguing mystery.... Give this to kids who think they don't like reading. It might change their minds." —*Booklist*, starred review

★ "Dryly hilarious first-person voice.... A kinder, gentler Wimpy Kid with all the fun and more plot."
—*Kirkus Reviews*, starred review

Praise for **My Life as a Stuntboy:**

"A fast-moving plot and relatable protagonist make this standalone sequel a good choice for boys."
—*School Library Journal*

"Fans of the first will be utterly delighted by this sequel and anxious to see what Derek will turn up as next."
—*Bulletin of the Center for Children's Books*

Praise for **My Life as a Cartoonist:**

"This entertaining read leaves some provoking questions unanswered—usefully." —*Kirkus Reviews*

"Great for reluctant readers (like Derek), this also neatly twists the bullying theme, offering discussion possibilities." —*Booklist*

JANET TASHJIAN

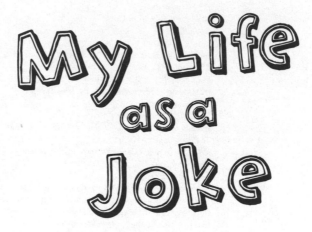

My Life as a Joke

with cartoons by
JAKE TASHJIAN

Christy Ottaviano Books
Henry Holt and Company
New York

Henry Holt and Company, LLC
Publishers since 1866
175 Fifth Avenue
New York, New York 10010
mackids.com

Henry Holt® is a registered trademark of Henry Holt and Company, LLC.

Library of Congress Cataloging-in-Publication Data
Tashjian, Janet.
My life as a joke / Janet Tashjian ; with cartoons by Jake Tashjian.
pages   cm
Summary: "Derek Fallon discovers all the angst that comes with being twelve—he just wants to feel grown up, but life gets in the way with a series of mishaps that make him look like a baby." —Provided by publisher
ISBN 978-0-8050-9850-1 (hardback)
ISBN 978-0-8050-9864-8 (e-book)
1. Children's art. [1. Maturation (Psychology)—Fiction. 2. Friendship—Fiction. 3. Middle schools—Fiction. 4. Schools—Fiction. 5. Family life—California—Los Angeles—Fiction. 6. Los Angeles (Calif.)—Fiction. 7. Children's art.] I. Tashjian, Jake, illustrator. II. Title.
PZ7.T211135Myd 2014
[Fic]—dc23

2013046395

Heh Heh
Heh Heh
Heh Heh

Henry Holt books may be purchased for business or promotional use. For information on bulk purchases, please contact Macmillan Corporate and Premium Sales Department at (800) 221-7945 x5442 or by e-mail at specialmarkets@macmillan.com.

First Edition—2014
Printed in the United States of America by
R. R. Donnelley & Sons Company, Harrisonburg, Virginia

10 9 8 7 6 5 4 3 2

For Jack Gantos,
with love and gratitude

A Time to Celebrate

"This is going to be a great year—I can feel it!" I watch the hands of the clock as they inch toward midnight.

Yesterday we stocked up on goodies: pepperoni pizza, strawberries and whipped cream, pistachios, coconut ice cream, double chocolate chip cookies, and celery. (I know that celery doesn't sound like much of a treat, but I

editor

checkered

dangle

like to take giant crunchy bites, let the stalk hang out of my mouth, and pretend I'm a newspaper editor in an old-fashioned movie smoking a cigar and barking out orders to a roomful of reporters. Don't ask.)

My mother wears a checkered blue dress she got on sale in the Beverly Center. She tells Dad and me how the dress was marked down four times—which is unfortunately the number of times she tells the story now. The silver earrings Dad gave her for Christmas dangle from her ears, and she wears pointy high-heel shoes; it's strange to see her in anything besides the comfortable flats she wears in her veterinary practice most days.

My dad excuses himself to run upstairs and change his shirt. He says it's because he's chilly but I think it's because in our jeans and T-shirts, we look more informal than Mom, and he knows how much she likes any excuse to dress up. I take the hint and sneak into my room to change.

informal

When I come back downstairs, my mother stops lighting the candles on the mantelpiece. "Derek, you're wearing your suit!"

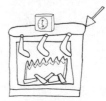

mantelpiece

The only other time I've worn this suit was to Mr. Mitchell's funeral last September. Mr. Mitchell was our next-door neighbor for the entire time we've lived in this house. His obituary said he died "after a long illness," but anybody in our neighborhood could've told you it was from a brain tumor. Ms. Carlton across the street organized an alternating weekly meal calendar so

obituary

Mrs. Mitchell didn't have to worry about cooking. Even though we and the other neighbors ended up cooking meals for three months, nobody complained. THAT'S how nice the Mitchells are.

I grab my lapels and spin around. "It's New Year's Eve!"

catapult

Somehow this coming year already seems different. I know I'm only twelve, but it's as if I'm about to catapult into feeling less like a little kid and more like an older one. I'll be a teenager soon, almost as cool as the upper classmen I sometimes watch from the corner of my eye at school. I could never talk with my friends Matt or Umberto about this. Carly, however, would love to sink her teeth into this subject. But the thought of discussing how mature we can be makes me whip off my suit jacket and start jumping on the couch. I grab the bag of confetti my dad went to three stores to find and toss handfuls around the room. My mutt, Bodi, barks and tries to jump onto the couch with me.

mature

confetti

"Hey, I thought we were waiting until midnight." Dad looks at my mother with his Something-Is-Wrong-with-Our-Son face.

"Happy New Year!" I jump off the couch and run into the kitchen to get my capuchin monkey, Frank.

"Derek!" My mother's voice is a bit louder than my father's. "I hope you're not taking Frank out of his cage."

But it's too late—Frank is now sitting on my shoulder, grabbing the confetti as I hurl it into the air.

overtired

"You might be a little overtired," my father says.

"It's only eleven thirty," I answer. "I'm not tired at all. In fact, I think we need more snacks."

My mother gazes at the half-empty trays of food we've been munching on for hours.

"We need to start the New Year with sliders," I suggest.

My parents look at each other, deciding what to do. On the one hand, it's late. On the other hand, they've been encouraging me lately to cook some simple meals.

"Okay," Mom finally says. "But wear an apron so you don't stain your clothes."

I take out the apron Dad uses to barbecue that says THIS GUY LOVES BACON and tie it around my waist. My mother gets a package of ground beef from the fridge, but I wave her away, saying I can do it myself. She scoops Frank into her arms and heads to the living room with my father.

I keep my eye on the clock as I form the beef into little patties. My mother pretends she's not looking into the kitchen, but I can tell she is. She doesn't realize that when it comes to hamburgers—even mini ones—I know what I'm doing.

It's ten minutes to midnight and the burgers are almost done when I'm suddenly faced with a crisis. WHERE IS THE KETCHUP? I rummage through the fridge, pulling out bottles and jars of condiments.

condiments

"Six minutes to go!" Dad calls.

From over my shoulder, I see my mom hold up her glass and my father pop open the bottles to

Champagne

prepare for midnight. (Champagne for them; sparkling cider for me.)

But before I can join them, an annoyingly loud BEEP BEEP BEEP fills the house.

I cover my ears with my hands as my mom runs into the kitchen.

"Derek, how many times have we talked about turning on the vent when you cook hamburgers?" She waves the dishtowel at the smoke detector. "Jeremy, can you shut this off?"

My father pokes the broomstick at the smoke detector while I hastily remove the now-burnt burgers from the stove. But the charred meat is the least of my problems—Bodi and Frank are going ballistic from all the noise. I try to seize Frank but he's in the living room, shrieking almost as loudly as the smoke alarm. The television only adds to the noise when the two hosts start the countdown.

"10! 9! 8!..."

Frank jumps into my arms, colliding with the remote on the way. He must've hit the channel button because the TV screen's now full of static and hissing noisily.

colliding

"What on earth is going on?" my mother shouts from the kitchen.

My father is on the stepladder, prying the battery out of the smoke detector. When it finally stops beeping, my mother hurries into the living room and presses different buttons on the three remotes until the screen returns to the special at L.A. Live.

stepladder

"There you have it!" the host announces. "A New Year's celebration for the books!"

"I think that's the most spec-tacular fireworks show we've ever seen!" The other host waves to the crowds kissing and having fun at the strike of midnight we missed.

"Happy New Year." My mom's acting happy as she makes the toast, but it's hard to miss the annoyance behind her smile. After we all hug, she puts Frank back in his cage and tells me it's time for bed.

I pull out the bag I have hidden behind the couch. "Here's what I was thinking—since Frank wears a diaper, he can be Baby New Year and Bodi can be Father Time." I hold out the sash and cotton-ball beard I made earlier.

"Bed," my father says.

Bodi follows dutifully behind me

dutifully

as I storm through the living room. I make a big show of grabbing a burnt slider from the pan to take with me upstairs.

I get into my pajamas and shove my suit underneath the stand of my aquarium. Why did I think this year was going to be different? Why did I think I'd finally get to be in charge of my own life? This year's going to be another 365 days of taking orders, going to school, doing chores, reading books, doing homework, etc., etc., etc.

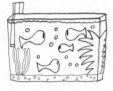

aquarium

They should change "Happy New Year" to "Ha Ha! You Think This Year Will Be Different but Don't Fool Yourself—You're Still a Kid."

Happy New Year? I don't think so.

Tomorrow's Not
Much Better

altered

I haven't watched parades on TV since I was little and my father doesn't follow football, so New Year's Day is surprisingly quiet. I don't know why I thought that just because the calendar changed, my daily life would be altered too. I take Bodi to the dog park same as I always do, pick up his poop the way I have for years. When I come back to the house, my mom's got on her woolen sweater and sunglasses.

"Come on, guys," she says. "We're off to Pasadena."

My dad and I wait for the other shoe to drop.

She answers our silent question by waving her arms like some guy on a runway guiding in planes. "The floats!"

At first I think she's talking about ice cream, but then I realize she wants to check out all the floats at the Rose Bowl. After the parade is done, they cordon off several streets where the town parks all the floats. Every year Mom wants us to see them up close, and every year my dad and I find a way to wriggle out of it.

"I think it's supposed to rain."

cordon

wriggle

I point to the sky, which is perfectly blue.

"The weather report said the winds are up through the pass," my dad adds. "They were warning people about driving in the Valley."

My mother puts her hands on her hips, clearly displeased. "I'm *not* taking no for an answer this year."

displeased

"We really *want* to go," my father lies. "I'm just worried about those winds. The meteorologist said they were blowing up to seventy miles per hour."

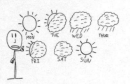

meteorologist

"Then pack your parachutes," my mother says. "And *I'll* drive." She scoops up her keys from the angel statue near the door. "Come on, guys. Chop, chop."

The mistake my dad and I made was not anticipating my mom's

annual plea earlier. Every year it's the same thing: She tells us how the floats are made with zillions of real flowers and how each town entering the parade spends months turning plants, herbs, stones, bark, leaves, and petals into painstaking designs. I'm sure thousands of people worked really hard on these floats; it's just not how I want to spend one of my days off from school. Isn't holiday vacation short enough as it is without looking at a carnation windmill?

painstaking

carnation

My dad throws on his sweatshirt and tucks his longish hair into the UCLA baseball cap I got him for Christmas. "Maybe after all these years of avoiding this, it'll be fun."

And maybe this is the year that reading becomes easy and I

suddenly turn into the smartest kid in my class.

"Come on," he says. "Mom does enough stuff for us. It's only fair."

I put on my own cap before Dad starts listing all the skateboard parks my mother drives me to.

My mother fills two travel cups with coffee and asks if I want to call a friend to join us. I tell her Matt is still at his grandmother's house and Umberto's at his uncle's.

inherited

"I bet Carly would love to see the floats up close," my mother continues. "Her mom's a landscaper. Carly probably inherited her love of plants."

I text Carly, shrugging to let my mother know I'm only doing it because she asked me to, not because it's a good idea. Carly texts me back immediately that she can be ready in ten minutes. That's a great un-girly thing about Carly— she's always prepared to walk out the door at a moment's notice if somebody's up for adventure. (Not that staring at a bunch of immobile floats is anybody's idea of exciting, but you get the idea.)

immobile

Since Carly's coming with us, my mom cleans out her SUV. It overflows with CDs (yes, she still uses them), tissue boxes, empty water bottles, and cardboard coffee cups. She tosses the trash into the barrel and brushes clumps of Bodi's hair off the backseat.

"Maybe YOU should enter the parade next year." I hold up several crumpled grocery receipts and empty granola bar wrappers. "You've got enough stuff in here to decorate ten floats."

"I think that's an excellent idea. Why don't we pick up an application while we're there today."

I whip around to see if she's kidding and thankfully she is.

My father climbs into the front seat with the fat holiday newspaper on his lap. It's mostly ads, but he'll read every inch of it anyway.

avid

It's so strange how my parents are both avid readers and I still struggle to read the books assigned in class. From a genetic point of view, shouldn't Mom's DNA combined with Dad's DNA almost GUARANTEE I'd be a good reader? It's a subject I'd like to read more about if—oh yeah—reading wasn't

genetic

such a chore. (I think that's what they call a Catch-22, a phrase that's probably based on yet another book I'll be unable to read.)

Carly climbs into the car as excited as if we were going to an all-you-can-eat-pizza-and-sundae party. She says hello to my parents, then gestures to her pants, which are some kind of stretchy, floral fabric. "I can't think of a better way to bring in the New Year than with flowers!"

Asking Carly to come along on a forced outing with my parents was a terrible idea.

forced

"My mother and I went a few years ago—it was great," Carly continues. "I'm going to take pictures."

My mom pulls onto the highway.

nudges

duration

"Then *lettuce* get on our way." She nudges my dad, who smiles at her pun.

I show Carly the new app on my phone to steer the conversation away from my mom's lame joke, but Carly's already taken the bait.

"I hear they use lots of vegetables," Carly says. "I can't wait to see what will *turnip*."

My mother laughs her big, horsey laugh, and I realize I'm now in this for the duration. Even worse, my dad decides to join in the punathon.

"The plum tree is ripe," he says. "It might be time to *prune*."

"I'm really taking a *lichen* to that tree," my mother continues.

Carly seems stumped, but of course she's not. "The apple crossed the street to get to the other *cider* the road," she says triumphantly.

triumphantly

Even from staring at the back of her head, I can tell my mom's super brain can generate a million of these stupid jokes. "I heard one palm tree asked another palm tree for a *date*," she says.

Dad puts his paper down. "I can't *cedar* forest for the trees."

"Come on, Derek," Carly says. "It won't take any *thyme* for you to catch up."

I stare out the window, trying to assess how many bones I'll break if I hurl myself out of the car at the next corner. I grab the stack of papers shoved next to Dad's seat.

assess

"*Weed* it and *reap*," my mother says.

Carly pounds on the armrest as if

that's the funniest thing she's ever heard. "Good one, Mrs. Fallon. I have to write some of these down." She starts rapidly entering the info into her phone.

preserve

"As if those jokes weren't lame enough, you want to preserve them?" I ask.

But in typical Carly fashion, she gets to the bottom of what I really think about all this. "Sorry," she apologizes. "We don't mean to make you feel left out."

Before I can lie and tell her of COURSE I don't feel left out, that the last thing I want to do is play their crummy little game, my mother interrupts.

"Carly's right, Derek," Mom says. "We might've gotten a little carried away."

"Thanks."

My mom can't help herself. "Yeah, with *fronds* like us, who needs *anemones*?"

Carly lets out a squeal of laughter; my father bangs his fists on the dashboard.

squeal

I am off from school for THIS? All I want is for everybody to *leaf* me alone.

A Parade That's Parked Isn't Really a Parade

grumbling

sprouted

Despite all my grumbling, it's a crisp, sunny day and even the five-block walk doesn't bother me. To be honest, it has less to do with the fresh air than with all the food carts of fried dough, kettle corn, and lemonade that have sprouted up on every street corner. By the time we get to where the floats are, I've eaten enough snacks to rival Halloween.

After that dopey car ride, I figured Carly would be holding hands with both of my parents, probably with them lifting her up and swinging her between them the way they used to do with me when I was little. But my parents are holding hands alone, walking leisurely behind us while Carly and I inspect the floats.

"The town hall on that float is constructed of rows of apples," she says. "And that dog is made out of bark."

constructed

I think about making a dog-and-bark joke, but the last thing I want to do is get everyone started on puns again, so I stand on the curb and look down the road. Thousands of people are ahead of us, also examining the floats. I had no idea this many people besides my mom would think a day like this was interesting or fun. The floats ARE pretty cool, but each one makes me wonder how people can spend so much time doing something that lasts just one day.

Even though I have notebooks and notebooks filled with drawings of my vocabulary words, most of my time at school is spent trying to get OUT of work, not volunteering for more. The thought of thousands of people offering to help put together these gigantic projects for the sake of town pride is pretty foreign to me.

volunteering

"We should volunteer next year," Carly suggests, as if reading my mind and trying to change it. "You and Matt are good with glue guns."

Carly knows full well that Matt

and I mostly use his mother's glue gun as a pretend ray gun. But the idea of working on one of these floats continues to grow. I imagine Matt and me on the astronomy float, each of us climbing farther to the top until we reach the marigold spaceships, squirting streams of glue across the sky. I picture other volunteers hurling handfuls of tulips and onions, screaming at us for ruining all their hard work.

astronomy

"Sounds awesome!" I say, and really mean it.

Carly's moved onto the next float—a library scene with stacks of books composed of tiny rocks. Even though it's vacation, it's still impossible to get away from books.

I put my hand to my eyes to shield them from the sun and try

shield

to find my parents. They're standing in front of a makeshift stage, watching three people in tights do something that looks like a cross between mime and ballet. The definition of what my mom thinks of as "art" is broader than anyone else's I know.

"So did you make a New Year's resolution?" Carly asks.

"Of course not. Did you?"

resolution

"My resolution is to read one book a week for the rest of the school year."

"One book a WEEK? Talk about setting yourself up for failure."

"What are you talking about?" she argues. "It's not that much more than I read now."

I knew Carly did a lot of reading outside of school assignments, but

I wasn't sure how much. A book a week?! The girl is a reading MACHINE.

The stack of library books on the float in front of us now taunts me even more. "The only way I could get through a stack of books like that would be to eat them."

"Then it's a good thing they're made out of lentils."

I don't tell her I thought they were pebbles.

"If you did make a New Year's resolution, what would it be?"

Carly looks at me with actual curiosity; the last thing I want is to disappoint her with some mediocre vow to improve myself. No, this is an opportunity to blow her away with how smart and self-aware I am. A chance to show how much

mediocre

I've grown up since we started hanging out together.

"This is the year I really figure out what I'm going to be when I grow up."

Carly nearly chokes on her gum. "Are you insane? You're only twelve!" She looks me up and down, trying to figure out if she should believe me. "Come on—be serious."

That's a phrase I hate, and I suddenly wonder why I invited Carly along. I mean, she's one of my best friends but half the time she's not happy unless everybody's brain is working at the same breakneck speed as hers. Times like this, hanging out with Carly is worse than doing errands with my mom.

Truth is, I haven't spent one second thinking about a New Year's

breakneck

resolution, let alone what I'm going to be when I grow up. But it was the first thing I could come up with on such short notice. "Besides, resolutions are what grown-ups make and never keep. They're not supposed to be for kids."

She snaps a photo with her cell of the Eiffel Tower and Taj Mahal made out of who-knows-what natural ingredients. "Never mind," she says. "It doesn't matter."

ingredients

But I can tell that Carly's disappointed, and in a strange way, I am too. It would be nice if I had one particular character trait to work on this year; it's not really too much to ask.

By the time we get to the float with the penguins made of tiny rosebuds, I've decided on a real goal for this year.

"My New Year's resolution is to take things more seriously."

Carly stops taking pictures. "You're making fun of me."

I tell her I'm not.

"You expect me to believe that you, Derek Fallon, are going to suddenly be mature?"

"That's exactly what I'm telling you."

"I don't believe you." She goes back to taking photos of the flowery penguins.

"I'm serious. You wait and see." The fact that Carly can't even IMAGINE me acting grown-up is kind of annoying.

She gives me a long, hard look. "Okay, Derek. THIS I've got to see."

"That makes two of us."

I never in a billion years would've verbalized a New Year's resolution if

verbalized

I'd known my mother was anywhere within earshot.

She's smiling and her arms are crossed as if I'M the one she's now watching perform.

That's what I get for opening my big mouth.

earshot

Back to School

The rest of the vacation goes by much too fast. Thankfully, my parents don't mention my resolution again, even when I set all the clocks in the house back half an hour just for the fun of it. Mom ended up missing an appointment to de-flea a Rottweiler, and Dad skipped a phone call at work, so needless to say, they were NOT happy. Even though I'd gone the extra mile and changed the time on the oven and the DVR, neither of them complimented my meticulous attention to detail.

The first person I run into at school is Umberto. He and I got together over break to go to the movies, but I'm shocked to see he's now sporting a crew cut.

military

"Are you joining the military? What's up?"

"I wanted something to mark the New Year," Umberto says. "Couldn't think of what else to do." He spins his wheelchair around me, checking out my latest duds. "Looks like somebody got new corduroys for Christmas, Mr. All Dressed Up."

corduroy

I don't tell him that wearing something besides jeans and one of my skateboard T-shirts is MY plan for the New Year.

Matt sneaks up behind me and grabs my new pants by the waist as if he's going to give me a wedgie. "All dressed up and nowhere to go," he says. "You got a big date with McCoddle?"

I fake-punch him in the arm. Ms. McCoddle's been teaching in our town since we were in kindergarten; even though she's fun with super-blond hair, the thought of trying to impress her with my new outfit is absurd. (That's not to say I don't look good, because I do.)

absurd

Matt tells us all about going to Six Flags and how his cousin got sick—twice—while riding the giant roller coaster. "He was sick as a dog after the first ride, but when I dared him to go on again, he did!" Matt shakes his head in disbelief. "He's my cousin and he's great, but the guy's a sucker for punishment."

Umberto fills us in on the computer program he worked on over vacation. It seems pretty complicated to me, but Umberto actually created a fun bowling game in less than a month.

"When you knock over the pins, it starts raining in the bowling alley," Umberto says. "It's pretty awesome, if I do say so myself."

Matt and I agree to go to Umberto's house this week to check it out.

"Nice outfit," Carly says.

I yell thanks, not sure if she's making fun of me or not. As she turns in to the classroom, Carly

samurai

announcement

shoots me a quick wink, which scares me more than ten samurai warriors charging down the hall with swords drawn. Is she goofing on me or do I seem more grown-up in these clothes? Somebody better explain what's going on because I don't have a clue.

"Okay, class." Ms. McCoddle leans against the board and faces us with a relaxed smile. "No more vacation. It's time to get back to work. But first, an announcement. We're having a toy drive."

"Hel-lo! Christmas is over!" Matt shouts through cupped hands.

Ms. McCoddle must've had a restful vacation because she shoots Matt another calm smile instead of reprimanding him. "It's not a holiday drive. This is for the new children's shelter. The Parent Association has pledged a playroom full of new toys, and they're looking for volunteers at all the schools. Anyone interested?"

pledged

Usually this is where Carly's or Maria's hand would shoot up before anyone else's. But Maria's still not back from vacation, and Carly's calendar is overflowing with so many extracurricular activities, she couldn't be on one more committee if she cloned herself.

extracurricular

"Any volunteers?" Ms. McCoddle asks again. "One of the boys for a change?"

Here it is, right in front of me— the perfect chance to show how grown-up I can be, to think about other people besides myself. As if to emphasize the point, Carly turns

emphasize

around in her seat, shooting me an expression that says, "WELL?"

"I'll do it," I tell Ms. McCoddle. "I'll be happy to."

brownnoser

From the seat behind me, Matt coughs "brownnoser" loudly into his hand.

Much to my eternal gratitude, Ms. McCoddle doesn't make a big deal out of me volunteering by turning it into some lame teaching moment. "Very good," she says. "I'll give you the contact information after class." She takes out her Language Arts textbook and tells us to turn to page 124.

Matt tosses papers at my head. When I turn around to look at him, he whispers, "Is the plan to keep all the good toys for yourself, especially the video games?"

Sooner or later I'm going to have to tell him this is all part of the new me. Hopefully, he'll like this version as much as the old one.

There's No F-U-N in the Word "Committee"

unnecessary

My mother, of course, makes an unnecessary fuss out of the fact that I volunteered to help the children's shelter. As expected, she brings up my New Year's resolution.

"I can tell this is going to be the year you really start to figure things out," she says proudly.

"It's not like I've been walking around CONFUSED for twelve

years," I say. "Besides, I'm not curing a disease. I'm just collecting toys."

"Well, I think it's a step in the right direction."

direction

"As opposed to what—the normal maze I walk around in?"

She ignores me as I hoped she would and goes back to paying bills.

Because the committee meeting is at my old elementary school, I skateboard over like I used to in fifth grade, stopping at the newsstand to buy enough candy to fill my pockets the way I did then too. It's nice that some things remain the same.

I can say the same thing about Mrs. Sweeney, still manning the school's reception desk. She's as tiny as a bird with giant tortoise-shell glasses. I always thought she'd make a great cartoon character. When she sees me, she gives me the same salute she did every day of my elementary school career. I have no idea how our routine started, but I take comfort in the fact that both of us recall it now. I head to the cafeteria kind of late, hoping the meeting won't last more than a few minutes.

recall

A woman is speaking to twenty other volunteers seated at the long wood tables. Mrs. Pankow, who always gave me extra gravy, holds up a spatula from behind the counter and waves. I wave back and sneak into the last row.

spatula

As I glance around the room, I realize I'm the only kid here. I thought Ms. McCoddle said there would be a volunteer from every school—is this another case of me paying only partial attention? I look around at all the moms and one dad; most are taking notes.

partial

"And here's our youngest volunteer," the woman in front says as she gestures toward me. She scans the papers clutched in her hand. "You must be Derek. Welcome."

clutched

I nod half-heartedly. This was a giant mistake.

"Does anyone have any questions so far?" the woman asks.

Yes. WHAT HAVE I GOTTEN MYSELF INTO?

half-heartedly

I politely raise my hand. "Sorry I'm late. Have you talked about what everybody's job is yet?"

She clacks over to me in the highest heels I've ever seen. Movie-star high heels, not normal-person

buffed

shoes. "Here's your handout, honey."

Her singsong voice has a trace of a New York accent, and her red nails are buffed shinier than the Mustang our neighbor Mr. Bosworth keeps under a tarp in his driveway.

"There are lots of categories— books, video games, DVDs. You're in charge of dolls."

"What?!"

But the woman plows ahead as if she hasn't heard me. "My cell and e-mail are on the bottom of the info packet," she says. "Feel free to give me a call with any questions. See you next week—and most of all, thank you!"

packet

Is this what happens when you stop for penny candy—you get stuck with the worst job on the planet?

(Maybe it was a bad idea to sit on the milk crate and read those comic books too.)

I approach the woman with the red talons and the skyscraper shoes. "Um, excuse me. I was just wondering if I could switch to the DVD or video-game group."

talons

"More fun than dolls, is that it?"

"I feel that's where I'd be most helpful," I answer.

"Sure. What kid your age wouldn't want to collect a pile of video games and DVDs? Sorry, Derek. You snooze, you lose. Dolls it is." She tilts her head and raises her eyebrows as if to say, *Yes, this is a teaching moment. I hope you're getting something out of it.*

I nod but my head isn't saying *Yes.* It's saying *I didn't learn a thing.*

reassign

I'm going to collect the crummiest, creepiest dolls I can find until you reassign me to a better group.

She gathers up her things, thinking that we're done.

We're not.

Ribbit

The next week, Ms. McCoddle points to a cardboard box in the back of the room labeled DOLLS in giant letters. "The head of the committee dropped this off. She said she hopes you'll have lots of donations for the meeting next month."

Not only do I have to go to another meeting with the woman with razor fingernails and stilts, but it seems

recruiting

I'm expected to cart dolls around all day too. I am DEFINITELY recruiting Carly to help me out with this.

But it turns out Carly's got her own activities to worry about, and Matt and Umberto want no part of what was supposed to be a great plan to be more grown-up.

"Why don't you put the box near your locker?" Ms. McCoddle suggests. "That way people know where to take their donations."

snicker

I'm usually too busy drawing at my desk to pay attention to the morning announcement, but when I hear my nemesis, Swifty, snicker over the intercom, I fear for the worst.

"Dolls! Dolls! Dolls!" Swifty announces. "Bring your new and gently used dolls to Derek Fallon this week. Derek loves to play with dolls and he wants yours!"

I slink underneath my desk, wishing I could disappear. What makes it worse is that Matt and Umberto are laughing along with the others.

slink

"Seriously," Swifty continues, "Derek is pretending to collect dolls for the new children's shelter. But he really has a giant doll collection at home."

Everyone in school can hear Principal Demetri running toward the mic.

"So bring all your Barbies, your American Girls, your Raggedy Anns. Derek wants to play with all of them!"

By the time Mr. Demetri yanks the mic away from Swifty, the whole school is laughing. This is why most people don't volunteer for things—that and the WORK.

The flyer the committee sent home last week must've done the trick because a few kids in my class—make that the girls—take out dolls from their desks and pass them down. Matt takes a stewardess Barbie and dances it across my desk. "Coffee, tea, or me?" he asks in a shrill voice. I grab the doll out of his hand and shove it under my chair with the others.

What a nightmare.

Just when I think things can't get any worse, Ms. McCoddle tells us to grab the handouts from our last class. *Please don't ask us to read out loud,* I think. *PLEASE!*

But things continue to slide into

shrill

the abyss. Not only is Ms. McCoddle making us read aloud but she calls on me first.

abyss

The story is about a rebellion in a big city, and there are lots of words I don't know. I realize I'm behind in my vocabulary illustrations and pray Ms. McCoddle doesn't stop and ask me to define any of those hard words.

rebellion

I look up at Carly who gives me a reassuring smile to keep going. I know I sound like I'm back in elementary school, but I put one word in front of the other until Ms. McCoddle thankfully asks Kevin to pick up where I left off.

On our way to science, I gather up my strength and ask Carly if I sounded like a baby. "Not everyone reads fast," she says. "Besides, it's

generous

approved

uneasy

about how much you understand, not how fast you read."

It's a generous bit of feedback, especially since my comprehension is almost as bad as my reading speed. At least I can make up for it in science, which I'm a little bit better at than English.

Ms. Miller is very excited and tells us that a grant she applied for got approved, so we're starting a new section. She passes around latex gloves with as much gusto as if she's handing out free money. I'm eager to hear what the new project is, but the way my morning's gone so far, I can't say I don't feel a bit uneasy.

She actually makes us close our eyes; when she tells us to open them, she points to trays of dead frogs. A few of the kids groan and say, "Ewwwwww." But Umberto, Matt, and I are totally psyched.

It's time to dissect frogs!

This Is a First

Ms. Miller has to tell Matt, Umberto, and me to stop playing with our dead frogs three times before she marches over wearing her mad-teacher face. I have no excuse except for the fact that a lot of kids are freaking out at their dead amphibian and it seems such a waste not to take advantage of it.

amphibian

Matt excuses himself to go to the restroom. When he comes back a few minutes later, I can see that he wasn't in the boys' room at all, but pilfering through the donation box instead. He holds up outfits a few of the dolls were wearing just minutes ago. Before you can say "Presto, chango!" we're dancing our frogs along the table in their new clothes. (I especially like the small fedora on Umberto's frog.)

pilfering

"BOYS!" Ms. Miller is not amused.

We disrobe the frogs, but not until Carly digs out her phone and snaps a quick photo.

disrobe

Ms. Miller runs through the dissection process step-by-step, asking us fifty million times if we have any questions. The scalpel is totally cool, and I can't wait for her to finish with the instructions so we can begin.

scalpel

When she tells us to pick a

formaldehyde

incision

partner, Matt and Umberto are already sitting together, so I pair up with Carly.

"You can really smell the formaldehyde," Carly says. "I'm glad Ms. Miller opened the windows." She gives my arm a nudge and tells me to stop poking the poor frog.

"His name is Gerald," I tell her. "He's from a large family in the Everglades."

Ms. Miller *finally* gives us the go-ahead to start dissecting. As much as I'd like to make the first incision, I decide to be a gentleman and let Carly do it—mostly because she beats me to the scalpel.

"I didn't think we'd be dissecting till next year," Carly says. "This is great."

As I watch Carly cut into the frog's abdomen, I suddenly get a whiff of the formaldehyde she's been talking about. I hold on to the corner of the table to catch my breath.

"Are you okay?" Carly asks, barely looking up.

I nod *yes* but feel my legs start to tremble. Maybe my problem is that I'm watching someone dissect instead of doing it myself. "Hey, how about giving me a turn?"

tremble

Carly hands over the scalpel, and I move in close to Gerald.

"You seem a little woozy," Carly says. "Why don't you sit down?"

woozy

"I've GOT this." Why is Carly treating me like a baby? I shoot her a look of annoyance, but when I turn back to the bench, my hand hits the

airborne

pandemonium

tray hard and suddenly Gerald is airborne.

I shout "NO!" as I watch the frog sail across the classroom, almost in slow motion. Matt and Umberto jump off their stools as Gerald glides above their heads.

"Incoming!" Matt yells.

In a split second, the class goes from quiet to pandemonium. Ms. Miller walks down the aisle, demanding to know what's going on. Just as Maria points to the flying amphibian, Ms. Miller finds out for herself when the frog comes in for a landing. On her blouse.

Anyone will tell you Ms. Miller is the most no-nonsense teacher at the school. So when she starts doing a rabid version of the chicken dance, the entire class breaks into laughter.

With all that hopping around, I watch in horror as the frog slides down her neckline and INTO Ms. Miller's blouse.

"Class! Stop laughing!" Ms. Miller shrieks, clawing at her shirt.

I look down at the empty tray in front of me. How did this happen? A waft of the formaldehyde hits me, and before I realize what's going on, I drop to the floor.

The next thing I remember is crawling into a sitting position.

A still not-happy Ms. Miller waits nearby, asking if I'm okay.

I shake my head to rearrange the cobwebs. "I've never fainted before."

fainted

She slowly helps me up. "Well, there's a first time for everything."

I look around the room. The rest

of the kids are all holding in their laughter.

As usual, Carly tries to get everything back on track. "It was probably the smell—it's pretty repulsive."

repulsive

"Maybe Derek passed out from all the excitement," Maria says. "Or maybe he was too afraid to dissect." Maria gives me a smirk. That's what I get for trying to scare her earlier with my dressed-up frog.

"Derek, sit down for a few minutes." Ms. Miller is firm, furiously rubbing her neck with a paper towel. "Everybody else, back to work."

Before he returns to his bench, Matt pulls me aside. "It was AWESOME! When you fainted, Ms. Miller bent down to see if you were okay, and the frog fell out of her shirt. Onto you!"

"You were wearing it like a brooch!" Umberto adds.

brooch

"That didn't happen!" But when I look around the room at my classmates, their giggling tells me Matt and Umberto are telling the truth. Now I'M the one grabbing for the paper towels.

I spend the rest of the class hiding behind Carly and poor Gerald. She's about to give me a turn with the scalpel, but Ms. Miller tells me to sit this one out and take notes instead. I get the feeling she's going to make me miserable for the rest of the school year.

Why did I think this was the year I'd become one of the guys the other kids look up to—not the boy who faints at a frog while everyone else takes part in a grown-up science class.

I hurry out of class as soon as it ends but Swifty and Joe are already at my locker. Joe picks a few dolls out of the collection box and holds them up in front of me.

"Oh no! It's a frog! I'm going to faint!" One by one, Joe sails the dolls into the air while Swifty fakes a girl's scream and jumps up and down like Ms. Miller.

All I want to do is go home. But before I do, I have to drag several boxes of DOLLS out to my dad's car.

Worst. Day. Ever.

Surprise Guests

At home, my mom is talking to a woman who looks familiar but I can't remember how I know her. The woman follows around a toddler who's exploring every inch of our kitchen. When I see Mrs. Mitchell come out of the bathroom, I realize the woman is her daughter who I met at Mr. Mitchell's funeral a few months ago. The toddler must be Mrs. Mitchell's granddaughter.

granddaughter

Mrs. Mitchell gives me a hug and thanks me for taking in her trash barrels every Thursday. I tell her it's no problem, because it isn't. She scoops up the toddler just as the girl's about to stick her finger into the electrical socket near the door. I take satisfaction in the fact that I'm not the most childish person in the room for a change.

I WANT CANDY!

childish

My mom peels a green apple as she talks. "I was just telling Mandy that we'd be happy to watch Olivia while she's helping Mrs. Mitchell pack."

"I still can't believe you're moving," I tell Mrs. Mitchell for the twentieth time this month.

"The house is too big for one person," she says. "And it makes more sense for me to move to Calabasas to be closer to Mandy and Olivia."

The only thing I know about Calabasas is that it's a big horse town. Mrs. Mitchell seems a bit old to take up riding but I guess there's a first time for everything. I'm in the middle of visualizing Mrs. Mitchell on a stallion, lassoing cattle, but am cut short by Olivia grabbing my cheeks. I quietly remove her hands and tell her I'm not made of Play-Doh.

stallion

Mrs. Mitchell flips through a stack of photo albums she must've brought with her. "Derek, come look at this."

I tear myself away from Olivia's grabby hands and look at the photo Mrs. Mitchell is pointing to. "Is that me?" I ask.

grabby

My mom looks over Mrs. Mitchell's shoulder and laughs. "I remember that day. You were covered in mud from head to toe and didn't want to change."

"You had to chase him up and down the street," Mrs. Mitchell adds. "Look at this one too."

She points to yet another photo of me as a toddler. If I'd known this afternoon was going to be a trip down Derek-as-a-Baby Lane, I would've stayed in school and fainted again.

Mrs. Mitchell points to a photo of her and Mr. Mitchell standing under an awning of the pinkest trees I've ever seen.

"There's nothing like the jacaranda trees in springtime," Mandy says.

jacaranda

"This was taken on Flower Street." Mrs. Mitchell looks wistfully at the photograph. I'm sure she's thinking about Mr. Mitchell more than the trees.

wistfully

My mother gives Mrs. Mitchell a gentle smile. "Flower Street—how appropriate."

"It's poetic too," Mrs. Mitchell continues. "This was taken where Flower Street turns into Hope."

Mandy gives her mom a smile that looks a little sad, then tells Olivia they have to go.

"Olivia likes you," my mom tells me later. "You'll make a great babysitter."

I was about to complain that my mom said WE were going to watch Olivia, not me alone, when I suddenly realize that neither Bodi nor Frank

interact

stucco

wounded

is in the kitchen. Mom says she wasn't sure how Olivia would interact with animals, so she put them in her office before they came over. I go next door to retrieve them and get us all a snack.

There have been a lot of changes in our neighborhood lately; in the past two months, four different people on the block have moved. I can understand Mrs. Mitchell wants to be closer to her daughter and granddaughter, but I also can't imagine anyone living in that beige stucco house but her.

As I get Frank and Bodi, I decide not to tell my mom about fainting in science class today. She'll just ask fifty million questions and want to "observe" me all night when the only thing wounded is my pride.

Besides, I've got a monkey and a dog—if they can't make you feel better, nothing can.

As I peel a banana for Frank, I realize he's making less noise than usual and wonder if he's already gotten into trouble. But he's lying on the rug next to Bodi—a real Christmas card picture—sucking on a pacifier. Between the diapers and the pacifier and the way he's cuddled next to Bodi, Frank could almost pass for a human baby. (Okay, a HAIRY human baby.) He fights me a little but finally surrenders the pacifier for a piece of banana. I know how possessive babies are with their things, so I walk over to Mrs. Mitchell's to bring the pacifier back.

When Olivia sees it, her eyes

pacifier

possessive

light up like Santa Claus is the new paperboy.

"We've been looking everywhere for that!" Mandy says. "Thanks so much for returning it."

I dangle the pacifier in front of Olivia, who tries desperately to grab it. "Frank was using it," I tell Olivia's mom. "I think he likes the pacifier as much as Olivia does."

She asks me who Frank is.

"Our capuchin monkey."

No one in the history of kids has ever cried louder than Olivia when her mother yanks the pacifier away just as she's about to pop it into her mouth.

"I rinsed it!" I say. "With soap!"

Olivia is now in a full-blown temper tantrum, complete with screaming, kicking, and tears.

tantrum

"Thanks for bringing this back," her mom says, shoving the pacifier into her pocket.

She hastily closes the front door, but even ten doors can't stop the sound of all that crying.

A Special Doll

sterilized

My parents spend most of the dinner conversation trying to explain why Olivia's mom wouldn't want Olivia sucking on the same pacifier as a monkey even though I kind of sterilized it. I guess it's like peeing in the shower; you're either someone who's comfortable doing it or you're not—and no amount of explaining can change your mind.

After dinner, Mom forces me to go through the notebook with my vocabulary words. She reviews the sentences and laughs at several of my drawings. Because she's being nice, I admit how embarrassed I was at school when I had to read out loud in front of the class. She doesn't try to make it better by pretending it was fine, just wrinkles her nose as if she understands how uncomfortable it must have been. Her support doesn't make that humiliating moment sting any less, but it does make me feel like maybe next time will be better. She also asks to see the comic strip I've been working on about a boy and his dog. She gives me some feedback about those drawings too.

pretending

Mom says she'll gladly give me a

ride to Santa Monica tomorrow afternoon to drop off the doll donations. It's been several weeks and the kids in our school really came through. I've now got five giant cardboard boxes overflowing with dolls for the shelter. Tall, skinny ones in fashionable clothes, old-fashioned baby dolls, dolls that talk—a little girl's dream come true. When one of the boxed dolls keeps falling out of the pile, I toss it on the couch. If Olivia's going to be at our house later, maybe she'll want to play with the doll while she's here.

fashionable

I'm hoping my mother's going to be the head babysitter with Olivia, but it turns out she and Dad have a meeting with their accountant, so I guide Olivia over to the shelf with the DVDs and hope she picks out a

accountant

good one. Even though *Toy Story* is older than I am, it's a classic and I don't complain when that's the one she chooses. I take the doll out of its box and try to make it sing along with the toys on TV, but Olivia pushes it out of the way as if this doll can't possibly compete with Buzz and Woody.

When Mrs. Mitchell and her daughter come back before the movie's finished, Olivia doesn't have to whine to get them to stay; they both take a seat and watch the end of the movie with us. Mrs. Mitchell sneaks me a little bag she picked up at the tiny chocolate shop downtown. Have I mentioned that I'm going to miss Mrs. Mitchell when she moves?

After the movie, I try one more

whine

time to get Olivia interested in the doll, but she brushes it away again. Her mom, however, takes a real interest.

"It's Baby Karen! I used to have her when I was little." she says. "This must be forty years old. I loved this doll!"

I explain how I'm not in the habit of collecting dolls and tell her about the committee I joined.

She gently sits the doll back on the couch while Olivia plays with the box. "I'm surprised someone donated her. I bet she's worth quite a few dollars by now."

I thank Mrs. Mitchell again for the candy and let Olivia pet Bodi. (Mom wisely put Frank's cage back in her office.) But as soon as they leave, I sprint to my dad's laptop. I do a quick search on eBay and am dumbfounded to discover three other Baby Karen dolls—all selling for over a hundred dollars! This doll doesn't seem that special but obviously the dozen people in an online bidding war feel differently.

dumbfounded

When my dad and I load the boxes of donations into Mom's car for the drive to Santa Monica the next morning, I "forget" to put Baby Karen back in the box and quietly hide her on the top shelf of my closet.

Ka-ching!

Matt Weighs In

christen

Matt agrees one thousand percent that Baby Karen belongs with us and not with the kids at the shelter. We even christen her Baby Goldmine.

"You already collected—what?—fifty dolls?" he asks.

I tell him sixty-two.

"That's PLENTY! It's more than enough for those kids to play with."

"Don't forget about the rest of the toys," I say. "The committee collected books, action figures, DVDs, and video games."

"How'd you get stuck with dolls?" Matt asks.

"I was late for the meeting."

"See!" he says as if that proves his point. "Now you HAVE to keep the doll."

His logic makes zero sense, but his zeal is contagious.

zeal

"Are you going to tell Carly?" Matt asks.

Telling Carly is pretty much the gauge for how guilty we feel. And as much as I've justified keeping Baby Goldmine, telling Carly seems like asking for trouble. I tell him no.

contagious

"What are you going to do with the money once you sell the doll?" he asks.

I know Matt really means what

are WE going to do with the money, but I tell him it's too soon to decide. On the one hand, the new Derek would find something mature and responsible to do with all that money—like maybe donate it to the children's shelter where it belongs. On the other hand, the old Derek will probably think of something great involving cheeseburgers, s'mores, pizza, and skateboarding— hopefully, all at the same time.

wealth

I'm so excited by the possibility of wealth burning a hole in my pocket that I don't even care when Maria and Nancy make fun of me again for fainting. It might've been a big deal before, but today I've got bigger fish to fry.

Look at All These Toys!

I never read the pamphlets that were handed out at the last meeting—surprise, surprise—but from overhearing a few people in the cafeteria today, the woman with the movie-star shoes is a big-shot fund-raiser named Debbie McManus, who works all over the city raising money for good causes. The woman next to me at the snack table says

overhearing

the shelter is lucky to have her. I'm not sure if these comments make me more or less afraid of Ms. McManus.

hobbles

When she finally hobbles over on her escalator shoes, I'm not sure what to say. "I never knew there were this many homeless kids in the city" is the best I can come up with.

"Be glad you're not one of them." Ms. McManus points to my chest with her bright pink fingernails. "We have to be grateful for our good fortune every day."

I know she's right but she's also scaring me, so I drift over to two guys standing by a table of DVDs. They don't see me standing behind them and whisper like they're part of a government conspiracy. "Nobody

conspiracy

would miss a few of these movies," one says.

The other one nods. "There are plenty of doubles here that would definitely not be missed."

I keep my eye on them to see if they pocket some of the DVDs. If they do, should I tell Ms. McManus? I suppose it's normal to think about lifting a few of the doubles; I mean, is it asking too much to be compensated for our time? After all, I "forgot" Baby Goldmine at my house. Maybe I'm just as bad as these guys are. Luckily, they meander over to the coffee table in the corner without taking anything.

compensated

Ms. McManus grabs me before I leave. "Thanks for collecting so many dolls. We need more kids like you trying to do their share."

fortunate

giddy

stashed

I nod but keep going.

"Thinking about those less fortunate than ourselves is one of the signs of growing up." She smiles sincerely, which makes me feel bad for running away every time I see her. "What a nice young man you are, Derek. Your parents should be proud."

It's the first time in my life that anyone's ever used the word *man* to refer to me and it makes me kind of giddy. I thank her for the compliment, trying to squash the picture of Baby Goldmine stashed in the top of my closet.

Auction Time

In the end, my desire for some fast cash wins out over my feelings of guilt, so Umberto and I go to Matt's to figure out how to use eBay. Turns out, you have to be eighteen with credit card information and other stuff that none of us have. But Matt's brother, Jamie, sells DVDs and CDs online and lets us use his account. Listing something on eBay may not look like a lot of writing and planning but for someone with lowly skills like me, even putting a paragraph together calls for real concentration. Of the three of us, Umberto's the best writer, so we leave the task to him.

A few minutes later, he reads us what he has. "Baby Karen doll, circa 1967."

"What does *circa* mean?" Matt asks. "It doesn't even sound like a real word."

"It means 'about,'" Umberto answers.

elaborate

"Then say that!" I never understand why people use elaborate—I mean, fancy—words when simple ones will do. I take over for Umberto and make up my own pitch for Baby Goldmine.

TOTALLY AWESOME BABY KAREN!
STILL IN BOX!!!!! WHAT A GREAT
DOLL!!!! SHE'S AMAZING!!!!
IN PERFECT CONDITION!!!! WHAT A
FIND!!!! JUST LIKE NEW!!!!! SHE CAN
BE YOURS TODAY!!!!!

"I think you can tone down the exclamation points," Umberto says.

Matt agrees and takes a photo of the doll in her box to add to the posting.

exclamation

We agree that for people who've never used eBay before we've done a great job.

While we wait for Bill to pick up Umberto in the van, Matt and I skateboard alongside Umberto in his wheelchair, hoping this is the day one of us finally beats him.

Umberto laughs all the way down the hill, victorious for another day.

victorious

OUCH!

For the next few afternoons, Matt, Umberto, and I continue to watch the online auction.

"I bet you make some serious cash," Umberto says. "There are four people bidding so far."

The three of us lower our voices when Carly approaches. She looks at us suspiciously, then shrugs. "I signed you up for the assembly later," she tells me.

assembly

"Why'd you do that?"

"The Student Council is always looking for assembly topics. I thought you could talk a little about volunteering for the shelter. Maybe it'll get other kids to volunteer for different causes later in the year."

Carly doesn't say it, but I know this is her way of supporting the new Derek. At first the thought of standing in front of the whole school terrifies me, but the more I think about it, the more I want to step into this new role. I tell Carly I'll gladly talk about volunteering.

"Yeah," Matt says, "you can tell everyone about all the OPPORTUNITIES available when you volunteer."

opportunities

It takes me a minute to realize he's talking about Baby Goldmine.

Carly, as usual, is much faster on the uptake than I am.

"What did you guys do?"

"Nothing!" Matt, Umberto, and I answer in unison.

mistrust

She eyes us with mistrust. "Seriously, what did you do?"

"NOTHING!" we repeat. I'd give anything to have the sixth sense for sniffing out lies that Carly has. It's almost a superpower. As a cartoonist, I might have to explore this possibility.

She finally drops the subject and tells me she'll meet me in the auditorium later. The rest of us head to P.E. None of us are happy when we see the setup in the gym: Mr. Walsh has attached ropes to the ceiling and filled the room with other equipment, like the balance beam

attached

and vaulting table. Even worse, there's another class in with ours— older kids who seem bored and bothered they have to perform feats of daring with squirts like us.

bothered

"Who ARE these guys?" Matt asks me. "And why are they butting into our class?"

Mr. Walsh explains that Mr. Costanzo is out, so today his class will be joining ours. I recognize a few of the kids from the pizza shop in the village; they're maybe a year older than we are but look much stronger and taller. We'll probably have our heads handed to us today, but Umberto sets the tone by performing twenty-five chin-ups in a row. The older kids half-heartedly join in the round of applause our class gives Umberto.

"Fallon, you're up." Mr. Walsh points toward the thick rope that's dangling from the ceiling.

I've climbed lots of ropes and ladders in my life, so I'm surprised that climbing this one is a lot harder than it looks. I feel a little better when I watch Matt on the next rope struggling as hard as I am.

struggling

"What'd Mr. Walsh do—soak these in slow juice?" Matt asks.

"Maybe we're just wimps," I tell him.

"Or maybe your I-want-to-be-mature-for-my-New-Year's-resolution is slowing you down."

I'm not the only one who's got growing up on his mind. Matt would never admit it but I notice him also checking out the older kids waiting for their turn on the ropes. Maybe talking to the whole school about the program at the children's shelter later will be a step in that direction. So is reaching the top of the rope and slapping the ceiling beam, which I finally do.

"Hey, Fallon!" Swifty calls from the ground below. "I can see your underwear."

"That's funny," I answer. "'Cuz I'm not wearing any."

Swifty isn't amused that I one-upped his joke. He looks around to make sure Mr. Walsh isn't watching, then grabs the bottom of my rope and jerks it sideways.

sideways

"Cut it out!" I yell, but not loud enough for Mr. Walsh to come running over and save me as if I'm a baby.

I'm horrified that Swifty is

intervention

burly

dismount

torturing me with these older kids here, a few of whom are laughing. After a few rough swings, I'd welcome any kind of intervention, even from a tough-talking, burly teacher like Mr. Walsh. Instead, Umberto's the one who comes to my aid, ramming Swifty with his wheelchair till he finally lets go of the rope. To make up for getting picked on, I show off with a fancy dismount. But instead of landing gracefully, I slam my face straight into the mat on the hardwood floor.

"Are you okay?" Matt asks, jumping off his rope the way you're supposed to when you're not showing off.

"I'm fine," I say. As soon as the words leave my mouth, I feel my lip starting to throb.

Mr. Walsh checks out my bottom lip and asks if I'm all right. I lie and tell him I am. Between this and the fainting episode, I feel like a giant klutz.

The older kids, of course, hog the showers after class. I don't take one anyway because I'm too busy staring at my lip in the steamy mirror.

"You might be puffy for a few days," Umberto says afterward. "It takes a while for swelling like that to go down."

swelling

"The assembly!" I'm not trying to make Umberto and Matt laugh but the *S*'s in *assembly* send them into fits of laughter.

"You sound like my little cousin," Matt says. "He has a lisp too."

lisp

"It's not funny!" But that sentence makes them laugh even harder. I get dressed as fast as I can and hurry to meet Carly in the auditorium.

As soon as she sees me, she knows something's wrong. "What happened to your lip? Did you get in a fight?"

deranged

I leave off the part about Swifty swinging the rope like a deranged Tarzan and tell her I fell off the rope in gym class. She scrunches up her face in an *are-you-okay?* kind of way that makes me feel a little better.

"Do I still have to do this? It's kind of difficult with a lisp." I try not to spit all over Carly as I watch the auditorium fill up with kids.

This is not good—not good at all.

A Tough Audience

Principal Demetri stands behind the podium to quiet everyone down. While he makes several announcements, pools of sweat gather in my armpits.

"Community service is an important part of your education," he continues. "Now Derek Fallon will tell us about the successful campaign for the new playroom at the children's shelter."

community

campaign

Hardly anyone applauds, which is fine—if I were sitting in the audience, I wouldn't either. I reach for the mic and pull it down to my height.

"Um...I really had lots of fun collecting toys for the shelter." It takes me a moment to realize there are too many *S* words in that sentence. I can already hear a few giggles from the back of the room. I look over to Carly standing backstage, smiling in her usual supportive way. All I want is to get this over with.

"It really didn't take that much time. I'd definitely volunteer again."

"You collected DOLLS," Joe pipes up from his aisle seat. "It's not like you did anything big."

secondary

This starts a secondary wave of

laughter. I lean into the mic. "I actually spent several weeks on this." That was WAY too many *S* words, and the audience responds by laughing even harder at my lisp.

I'm about to hightail it off the stage when Principal Demetri grabs the mic and faces the audience, especially Joe who's sitting directly across the aisle from Swifty. "Do you think this is funny?" the principal asks.

The room gets quiet quickly. Most students at our school like Principal Demetri, but anyone can tell you it's not a pretty sight to get him angry. I edge my way to the safety of the curtain; Principal Demetri, however, stops me in my tracks.

"One of our students joins people across the city to help out a nearby

graffiti

vandalism

escalates

shelter—a CHILDREN'S shelter, I might add—and you think that's a joke?"

Mr. Demetri is working himself up into the voice he uses whenever he finds graffiti or vandalism on school property. All I want to do is leave the stage before his anger escalates. Carly looks as worried about the blowback as I am.

Mr. Demetri puts his arm on my shoulder as if he and I are in this together, which we clearly are not. I lean away from the principal but it's too late.

"I'm going to recommend all students do community service at the middle school the way they do at the high school. Thank you, Derek—you've given me a good idea here today."

I look out to the sea of faces; NO ONE is smiling, not even Matt and Umberto, who look downright glum. You don't have to be a fortune-teller to see how this will play out—with the entire school hating me for adding one more job for us to do.

glum

"In fact," Principal Demetri continues, "I think we could use a little more community around here. Everybody stand up. We're all going to sing 'The Star-Spangled Banner.'"

The audience reluctantly rises. All I want to do is disappear.

Mr. Demetri hands me the mic, which I politely refuse. He insists. "Derek, why don't you lead us?"

I take a big gulp and find Matt and Umberto. Matt just stares at me wide-eyed while Umberto looks

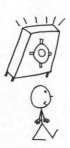

oblivious

about ready to wheel himself out of the room.

I don't get any farther than "Oh, thay can you thee" before the entire auditorium erupts in laughter. Principal Demetri seems oblivious to why everyone is laughing and bangs the podium to settle the room down. By the time I get to the song's climax, Carly looks like she might die from embarrassment on my behalf.

"Oh thay doth that thtar-thpangled banner yet wave ..."

When I hit those long, final high notes, the school breaks into hysterics, not applause. I race off the stage with Carly right behind me.

I lay into her as if she just ran over my dog—AND my monkey.

"This is YOUR fault. You and your stupid ideas—wanting me to address the whole school. What were you thinking?"

I feel my face flush with anger, but Carly's face is now as red as mine. "I was just trying to help you with your resolution! You were the one who wanted more responsibility."

"Well, thanks to you, I'm the school joke!" I kick the wall but it's concrete and the only thing I hurt is my foot. I hop on one leg all the way down the hall.

If this is what happens when you try to be a grown-up, lesson learned.

flush

Acting Mature Was an Immature Idea

The fat lip and lisp end up sticking around for several days. My mother thinks it's cute, my father thinks it's funny, but I am not amused. Every day at school SOMEBODY starts singing "The Star-Spangled Banner." And if they're not giving me grief about my lispy song, they're frowning about the possibility of more community service. Nothing in my life is working...nothing. Except maybe the turnout for the Baby Goldmine auction.

With two days to go, the bids are already up to ninety-eight dollars. I can't imagine anyone in his or her right mind paying a hundred dollars for a stupid doll, but according to the list of bidders, there are at least eight of these Baby Karen fanatics. Hey, knock yourself out! The higher the price, the better for me.

fanatics

I'm surprised when I open the door after school to find Mrs. Mitchell dropping off Olivia for a few hours. My mom has a full day of animal appointments and forgot to tell me Olivia was on my schedule today. Here's ANOTHER reason I can't wait to grow up—to be in charge of my own time, not have

jam-packed

bonkers

days jam-packed with stuff other people want me to do. Mrs. Mitchell leaves a bag full of crayons, paper, and board books, and tells me she and her daughter will be back in two hours. She thanks me profusely as she leaves.

Because I didn't know Olivia was coming, I didn't hide Frank. Olivia goes bonkers when she sees a capuchin monkey sitting in a cage on the counter. She pleads for me to take Frank out but I firmly tell her no. As much as I don't want to spend the next two hours babysitting, it feels good to be the one GIVING orders for a change, instead of being on the receiving end of all those rules.

I can't blame Olivia for not taking no for an answer. If I were two years old, I'd be jumping up and down to play with a monkey too. She begs, she whines, then she starts crying. I already want this baby-sitting job to be over, and Olivia hasn't even been here a full minute yet.

substitute

I try to substitute Bodi as a fun animal playmate, telling her what a great dog he is and how much his tail will wag if she pets him. However, her only interest in Bodi is as a stepladder; she climbs over my poor dog to get closer to Frank. I drag the crying toddler and Frank's cage over to my mother's office. I want to barge into Mom's examination room and complain, but she's in the middle of giving a pug stitches, so I head back to our house with the sniffling Olivia.

barge

My first thought is to text Carly to come over and help. I can't ask her, though, because we haven't really made up from our little fight at the assembly last week. I also know she'd just end up telling me that boys can babysit just as well as girls and I don't need her help.

I bring down a pile of picture books from my room and sit Olivia on the couch. Because of my reading disability, I still read a lot of picture books. There are a few I forgot about, and I find myself happy to discover them again.

We read for a little while until Olivia jumps off the couch and starts foraging through the box near the front door.

foraging

She holds up the stupid fishing hat that my father wears when he wants to annoy my mother. "I want the monkey to wear a hat!" Olivia shouts.

I tell her Frank's not here but even if he were, there's no way he'd wear a hat. (I don't tell her I've made him wear hats plenty of times.)

"I want the monkey to wear a hat!" she repeats, even louder.

I tell her again that Frank will NOT be wearing a hat today.

She holds out the hat. "YOU wear it."

"That's not going to happen."

She tosses me the hat and crosses her arms defiantly.

I almost start laughing because I remember having hundreds of tantrums of my own when I was little. As obnoxious as Olivia is being right now, I have to give her credit for persistence. I pick the hat off the floor and put it on.

persistence

overgrown

rambunctious

"YOU be the monkey!" Olivia yells, this time with delight.

I don't need a lot of convincing to start jumping around the room like an overgrown capuchin. Olivia joins in the act and leaps around the room with me. Unfortunately, she gets a little too rambunctious and her cup hits the floor, spilling all over me. I grab some paper towels and wipe the floor and my pants while Olivia continues to jump. I just hope that pretty soon she'll collapse in a state of exhaustion.

When I hear a knock at the front door, a wave of relief floods over me that Olivia can finally go home. But it's not Mandy; it's one of the older kids from school who joined our gym class. I suddenly realize I'm wearing a stupid hat and my pants are soaking wet.

This kid wears a cool vintage T-shirt with a Slinky on the front, and he's holding a skateboard that looks homemade and superfast. Even though I've whipped off the hat, he still looks at me warily. "Um, my name's Steve. I just moved in next door. The people we bought the house from said a skateboarder lived here."

warily

"That's me. I'm Derek." I try to figure out if I can salvage this horrible first impression. The last thing I want is for Steve to think I hang out with two-year-olds, so I try to block Olivia, who's still singing and dancing around the living room.

"You're the kid to blame if we have to do community service," Steve says. "The kid with the lisp."

I explain that I don't have a lisp

and if we DO have to do community service, it won't be because of me.

Steve sticks his head through the space between us, checking out the house. "Your bungalow looks the same as ours from the outside, but the inside's totally different."

bungalow

"I know—Mrs. Jacobson would've wallpapered the inside of the garage if Mr. Jacobson let her."

Steve lets out a little laugh that I take as a good sign—until Olivia dashes over and points to my pants. "Derek did pee-pee!"

I roll my eyes at Steve, trying to defuse the humiliating situation. "I obviously did NOT pee my pants. She spilled her juice all over me."

"No!" Olivia yells. "Derek went pee-pee!"

I give Olivia a little shove into

the living room and Steve takes a step back. "Anyway, I just wanted to say hi." He grabs his skateboard and slowly heads down the walk. I'm embarrassed to admit I chase after him like a hungry puppy.

I point to the board he's about to jump on.

"Hey, nice deck. Did you make it yourself?" But Steve's already on his phone, moving to the next thing on his teenage agenda. I watch my cool, A-list neighbor disappear down the street.

agenda

Back inside, Olivia has found my markers; her face and arms are now covered with a rainbow of colored streaks. It's one of the worst afternoons of my life—until I get a text from Matt, telling me to call him ASAP.

timidly

potential

"The auction just ended," he tells me on the phone. "Guess how much you got for Baby Goldmine."

"A hundred dollars?" I ask timidly.

"There was a huge bidding war in the last few seconds," Matt says.

I cross my fingers and ask him to tell me the final price.

"Two hundred thirty-two dollars," he says.

Suddenly losing a supercool potential friend and having to baby-sit a crazy toddler fade into the background. "DID YOU JUST SAY TWO HUNDRED THIRTY-TWO DOLLARS?"

"And the woman already paid." Matt pauses for effect and I can picture his canary-eating grin from three miles away. "Jamie's got a special business account where he gets the money right away. So come over and get your cash!"

I pace around the living room until Olivia's mom FINALLY comes to pick her up, then jump on my board to Matt's.

Did I mention I just made two hundred thirty-two dollars?!

I've Never Held This Much Money

instructions

Before Jamie forks over the cash, he makes sure we follow the shipping instructions to send Baby Goldmine to the person who purchased it: a woman from Memphis named Nancy. So Matt and I race back to my house, find a box the right size, and carefully prepare the package. We get a bit distracted by the Bubble Wrap, tap dancing on the plastic to make loud explosion noises. My father sticks his head out of his office with his phone to his ear and shoots us a look to knock it off. We do, not because we're bothering him but because we've popped all the bubbles. I use my best handwriting to address the label and even stick a note inside that says "THANKS!" After we show Jamie the receipt from the post office, he hands over the money.

receipt

Then Matt and I skateboard to the bank with my mom's ATM card to turn all the larger bills into ones. We then proceed to act out scenes we've watched in a million movies where lottery winners throw money into the air like confetti and roll around the floor in piles of cash.

massive

But when you spread it all over the floor of your basement, it's not like the massive piles you see in movies. That's not saying Matt and I don't enjoy every minute of throwing around all that cash because we do.

"You know we're not splitting this," Matt says. "The money's yours, fair and square."

It's nice of Matt to say, especially since all our ideas so far involved the word WE.

"I'm serious," he says. "If you want to spend this money on a new board or throw it into your savings account, that's fine with me."

I tell him thanks, but we're having so much fun thinking of possibilities that I don't want to stop. Matt suggests going to several amusement parks—there are tons of them within an hour of L.A.

"Or a party on the beach," I propose. "We can play volleyball and eat sushi."

Matt looks at me as if I just suggested we go to the zoo and club koalas with our skateboards. "You want to spend your money on RAW FISH?"

"It was just a suggestion."

"What's gotten into you? Next, you'll be showing up at school smoking a pipe and wearing an ascot."

ascot

"You LIKE sushi!" I pray Matt doesn't carry my whole mature thing too far. What am I talking about? It's Matt—of course he will. But he thankfully comes back around to brainstorming ideas.

"Maybe we can pay Heinz to take us to the best surf spots," he adds.

Heinz is Carly's surf instructor who we've all taken lessons from.

holler

"We should TOTALLY do that. Stick our heads out his sunroof and holler at people all the way to Zuma!"

By the time we finish, I have a list three pages long. How's THAT for extra writing credit?

A Second Impression

On my way to school, I bring Mrs. Mitchell's barrels up to the top of her driveway. From behind the blue recycle bin, I spot Steve next door hopping on his board. I haven't seen him since the Olivia incident. Rolling around on all that money must've given me extra confidence because I don't think twice about approaching him now.

"Hey, are you on your way to school? I can grab my board and join you." It's not till I finish talking that I realize he's wearing earbuds and hasn't heard a word I said.

Steve pulls out his earbuds and I repeat my offer. I try not to look disappointed when he tells me he's picking up some friends on the way. I'm about to sulk my way underneath Mrs. Mitchell's aloe plants but then Steve turns back to me.

sulk

"Hey, I'm having some friends over tomorrow night if you're around."

I try to contain myself and not jump up and down like a friendless mutant.

mutant

"Sure," I answer. "Tomorrow night is good."

"Cool." Steve jumps on his board and heads down the street.

Okay, I've definitely had some missteps this year, but between Steve's party and the cash I got for Baby Goldmine, things are looking up.

I suddenly notice Mrs. Mitchell outside in her pajamas. I ask if she's looking for the newspaper.

She seems surprised to see me but gives me a wide smile. "The garden's so pretty, isn't it?"

As I agree with her, I notice Mrs. Mitchell is barefoot on this chilly morning. I'm not sure why, but she seems like she needs protecting, so I guide her back to the porch.

"Derek Fallon, you're such a good boy."

"Young man," I correct her.

"A young man who'd like to take a warm cruller to school?" She holds on to the rail for support and goes

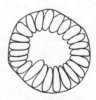

cruller

inside, emerging a few minutes later with a cookie sheet of warm pastries. She removes a cruller from the pan with a napkin just like the professionals in the doughnut shops. She's like my grammy back in Boston—nothing makes her happier than finding someone to savor her food.

savor

I thank Mrs. Mitchell for the cruller; she thanks me for taking in her barrels. Our relationship is very equitable. I check to see that she's safely inside before I leave.

equitable

The cruller doesn't even make it to the stop sign as I slalom down the street to school.

A Reason Not
to Brag

I try not to mention the party invitation to my friends, but my mouth has a mind of its own and before I know it I've told Carly, Umberto, and Matt—all before first period.

invitation

"Wow," Carly teases. "Hanging out with the older, new kid next door."

"Maybe we should go to the party with you," Matt suggests. "In case everyone ignores you and you're in a corner all alone."

"It might be good to have backup," Umberto agrees. "Parties with kids you don't know can stink."

"I was the one who was invited," I tell them. "I'll check it out and report back."

"There'll probably be lots of girls there," Carly says. "OLDER girls, pretty girls, new girls."

stalk

"Girls you can get crushes on who'll ignore you for the rest of the year while you stalk them in the halls," Matt adds.

squelch

"Girls you can pretend to run into who make fun of you behind your back." Umberto tries to squelch his laughter.

"Girls you better not spend the Baby Goldmine money on," Matt whispers.

"I'm leaving now. Good-bye!" I shake my head and hurry toward my locker. Sheesh! What a mistake THAT was.

But I can't complain too much—in their situation, I'd be doing the same thing. I also can't help feeling a tiny bit proud; with this party invitation, all the work I've been doing to try to appear a little more mature is obviously paying off.

whistling

Later, I'm practically whistling around the house, which immediately makes my mom suspicious.

"What are you so excited about?" she asks.

I tell her nothing but the smile on my face gives me away.

"Okay, spill." She crosses her arms, her smile matching mine.

I play hard to get for a moment, then tell her about Steve moving into the Jacobsons' house next door, how he's almost fourteen and having a party tomorrow night that he invited me to.

"Very nice," she says. "I haven't seen his parents around. Maybe we can invite them over for dinner."

I can't hide my exasperation. "Can't I have a friend first without dragging the whole family into it?"

"Of course. We can meet them later." She shoots me another smile. "If I need you tomorrow night, I can always go over and get you—maybe in my gardening clothes or when I clean up after a carsick dog."

"Very funny."

"I'm sure it'll be fun. Let me know if you want to bring anything."

What is my mother thinking—that I'm going to knock on Steve's

exasperation

door with a platter of appetizers? But after she says it, I wonder if I AM supposed to bring something. What's appropriate for a teenage party? A bag of chips? A bottle of soda? The bottle makes me think of spin the bottle, which brings on a colossal case of anxiety.

appetizers

anxiety

Mom's mind-reading antennae awaken. "What's going on?"

"Nothing!"

awaken

She rubs my back reassuringly. "I know you and your imagination, Derek. Don't take a simple invitation and turn it into some overblown event in your mind."

overblown

I HATE it when my mom crawls inside my brain. To change the subject, I take Frank out of his cage and head to the living room couch. Bodi follows, as he always does. I

dialogue

flip to one of the many movies I've been saving on the DVR and click on the one with the most car chases, the most explosions, and the least amount of dialogue.

The last thing I want to do right now is think.

OOPS!

I am mortified to admit how long it takes me to decide what to wear to Steve's party. In my entire life, I've never spent ten seconds deciding what to wear, never mind ten minutes. (If I'm being really honest, tonight it's more like fifteen.) In the end, I decide on one of my skateboard T-shirts and my jeans. Before I switch off the light, I take

mortified

DELJUBM

jumbled

one more look at the wad of cash I've hidden between my jumbled pairs of socks. It's taken a lot of discipline, but I haven't spent a dollar yet.

I don't want to be the first one at the party, so I ride up and down the street on my bike until several other kids have gone into the house. Older kids, cooler kids. I put back my bike, take a deep breath, and knock on Steve's door.

"Hey, Derek! Come on in." Steve—who remembered my name!—seems genuinely happy to see me.

He introduces me to the kids playing video games in the main room, then leads me to the kitchen.

"You want a soda or some chips?"

Even though I came empty-handed, I congratulate myself for guessing the correct items to bring

congratulate

to a teenage party. I grab a handful of chips and a soda can.

"This is my little brother, Taylor. He's five." He gestures to a kid with a runny nose, playing with wooden trains in the corner of the room. "My parents won't be back till ten and said I had to babysit him. I thought since you babysat other kids, you can watch him for a while."

The sad truth of the situation starts to sink in. "You invited me to your party so I could babysit for your brother?"

Steve looks at me with a quizzical expression. "You thought I invited you to hang out with my friends?" He hands me a stack of picture books. "Taylor loves the one with the kitty. Maybe you can start with that after you finish playing trains."

On his way back to the living

quizzical

room, Steve gives me a quick wave. "Thanks a lot, Derek."

I stand in the tiled kitchen, feeling as young and alone as Steve's little brother. This is outrageous! How arrogant and inconsiderate!

inconsiderate

But here's another sad fact I'm embarrassed to admit:

I stayed.

Lying to Friends and Family

For a little kid, Taylor ends up being a tolerable playmate. We play trains, we read picture books, I even come up with a story about a zombie platypus that he makes me repeat three times. In between games, I watch the older kids hang out in the living room. I recognize Brenda Osborne and Melissa Hamilton, two of the most popular girls in school. Melissa is telling a story that has

tolerable

several of the others riveted. Steve and Bill Hernandez shout at the screen during their video game. Several other kids mill around the room, talking or sharing photos on their phones. From the outside, it seems like a fun party—not that I'd know from my hiding place in the kitchen.

As I try to get a better look at Brenda, I notice that Taylor has taped large pieces of paper to the wall. I give him a disapproving look and then tell him that he'll probably be in tons of trouble when his parents get back home.

creative

"My mom likes it when I'm creative," Taylor says without looking up.

I tell him that I like to draw too, and Taylor hands me a thick purple marker. "Can you teach me how to make cave paintings?" he asks.

I have to admit it's nice to be wanted for something besides babysitting. "Well, if it's a cave painting, we should use red or brown."

Taylor runs upstairs to get more markers. When he returns, I draw a small stick-figure man and a mammoth next to Taylor's doodles.

mammoth

He takes a marker and draws two men with spears; I follow with three horses. It doesn't take long for us to cover most of the walls.

"Wait!" Taylor suddenly runs upstairs again and comes down wearing a Tarzan-like leopard skin. "We can be real cavemen! You can wear this!" He hands me a long piece of cheetah-print fabric that I tell him I'm NOT going to wear.

"It's from the den," Taylor says.

signals

"No one cares." He signals to the living room.

I take off my T-shirt, throw the small blanket over my shoulders, let out a few grunts, and continue drawing. Before long, we've wallpapered the kitchen full of men, women, and animals.

"What are you DOING?"

I turn around to find Steve and everyone else from the party crowded in the doorway. I explain that I'm giving Taylor some art lessons—caveman style.

Steve's face grows red as he rips one of the papers from the wall, which is now filled with the shadows of our cave paintings. "Those permanent markers bled through the paper. My mother's going to KILL me!"

I look over to Taylor, who shrugs innocently.

"And you're wearing my mother's scarf!" Steve yanks the cheetah print off me, then starts furiously scrubbing the wall with a sponge.

As I slip my shirt back on, I shoot Brenda and Melissa a weak smile but they continue to stare at me blankly.

menace

"OUT!" Steve says. "You're a menace, a joke! I'm going to get grounded because of you!"

I have to fight the urge to shout, "I'm not a loser. I have two hundred thirty-two dollars in my sock drawer!" Taylor gives me a big wave when I leave; no one else says a thing.

I slip into my house even more quietly than the time Matt and I went nighttime skateboarding with flashlights. But the sneakiest ninja in the world can't get past my mother, who spots me faster than a hawk.

"How was the party?"

I look at her face with its mixture of anticipation and kindness, and I lie. I tell her it was great; I tell her I made lots of new friends.

lingers

"I'm glad you had fun." She tousles my hair and says she'll see me in the morning. She lingers for a moment on the stairs, then heads back down to the kitchen.

Before I go, I find Bodi and make sure he follows me up to my room. Tonight's definitely the kind of night a kid needs a dog to sleep at the bottom of his bed.

I keep myself busy all weekend, doing family stuff to avoid the texts from my friends. When I finally see everyone Monday morning, Steve's party is the first topic of conversation.

"Well?" Carly stands on her tiptoes as if the party suddenly caused me to grow three inches and she's trying to catch up.

Matt and Umberto also wait for my answer.

I'd planned on lying like I did with Mom but it hardly seems worth the effort. Telling the truth doesn't seem like a good option either. I eventually grunt a few syllables and say the party was fine.

Carly won't let the subject drop. "Come on, be more specific!"

specific

"Yeah," Matt adds. "Are you going to dump us for your big, cool friends now?"

Umberto spins his wheelchair

in front of me, blocking my escape. "Come on, dude. Spill the beans!"

What am I supposed to do—tell my friends how I got outsmarted by a little kid and humiliated myself in front of every older kid there? I spare myself the embarrassment, dodge Umberto's wheelchair, and hurry down the hall.

outsmarted

"You can't escape!" Matt calls.

"We'll find you!" Carly adds.

"See you at lunch!" Umberto says.

stomachache

I think about faking a stomachache but gather the courage to stick it out the whole day. (Although I do dive into the media center to hide when Brenda Osborne heads down the hall after science.)

My friends corner me in the

cafeteria later and I have no choice but to answer them. I tell them the party was fun although I mostly just hung out with Steve.

"So when do we meet him?" Matt asks. "Where does he skateboard? We can go."

Matt's not teasing me; he's trying to make an opening in our group for a new member. A wave of good thoughts washes over me. I already HAVE cool friends. Why am I looking for new ones? And I immediately know what I'm going to do with my two-hundred-thirty-two-dollar windfall: stop stalling and plan an incredibly awesome day for my REAL friends.

windfall

The Event of
the Year

entertain

I make a giant list of possibilities for great ways to entertain my friends. Paintball and all the grilled cheese sandwiches you can eat? Laser tag and BLTs? Beach party and smoothies? I finally zero in on a few final choice.

First on my list is a Tony Hawk appearance in San Diego. It's two hours away but Tony has been

Matt's and my skateboard idol since before we jumped on our first boards. He's the most famous skate-boarder in the world, which means Matt and I are in the company of millions of others who love to watch Tony perform. I'm disappointed to discover that the tickets to his show sold out the first day.

Plan B is something else Matt, Umberto, and I have talked about several times. It might not be Carly's cup of tea, but she's usually game for new things. After getting the company's name online and having a conversation with the manager, everything is set to go. Until I realize I haven't asked my parents.

Figuring out how I got money for a party takes some brainwork—and a giant lie. I make up a story about

brainwork

winning a raffle the children's shelter had for all its volunteers and that I wanted to spend the winnings on my friends. (At least that part is true.) I can tell my mom's about to grill me for more details but she gets an emergency call to help a poodle that broke its leg in the canyon. (Lucky for me; not so lucky for the poodle.)

I gather my friends at my house after school and tell them I have an announcement. Matt bangs a drumroll on the steps with his hands.

"I've planned something amazing for us to do next weekend."

They each make a few off-the-wall guesses before letting me reveal the answer.

reveal

"I'm renting a Monster Truck."

Matt and Umberto go nuts.

"When I talked to the guy at the

rental place, he said he can use the driveway."

Carly looks down the road at all the parked cars lining our street and asks if the Monster Truck will fit.

flatbed

"The guy said it'll be on a flatbed," I answer. "He suggested we ask a few of the neighbors to move their cars when he pulls in."

"But we won't be able to drive it," she says. "What do we do—just sit on it?"

Matt and Umberto look at her like she has ten heads. "We take pictures of ourselves on it!" Umberto says.

Matt shakes his head at the lameness of Carly's question, but she continues her impression of a stick-in-the-mud anyway. "Where did you get the money?" she asks.

This time Matt and Umberto are

silent, putting on their straight faces as I tell Carly the same raffle story I told my parents.

She nods thoughtfully. "It's not like we need to do something expensive to have fun."

Carly now sounds like a mini-Mom, and we all tell her she's wrong.

Here's what I DON'T tell Carly: that as much as I want to share the Baby Goldmine windfall with my friends, I also can't wait to rub my neighbor Steve's nose in the fact that he isn't invited to my party. Having an awesome Monster Truck in the driveway while Steve watches from the curb DID play a small part in my decision. Vengeful? Maybe. I'm just hoping it lessens the feeling of humiliation whenever I think about babysitting his little brother instead

vengeful

of hanging out with Steve and his friends.

"I just want you to know—this party's all on me," I tell my friends. "I pay for everything, you just come, okay?"

Carly's got second thoughts. "We can all chip in," she suggests.

"I want you to promise you won't spend a penny," I tell them.

"No argument from me," Matt says.

Umberto agrees.

Before she leaves, Carly pulls me aside. "Want me to make sure everything's okay with the rental? I know how you are with details."

"Stop treating me like a baby! I may not be able to read a book a week but I can do SOME things independently."

independently

"I just want to help."

"I know you do." I tell her I'll see her at school.

As if to prove she's not a wet blanket, Carly chants "MONSTER TRUCK! MONSTER TRUCK!" all the way down the driveway.

Not Exactly What I'd Planned

The Monster Truck is already half an hour late, but Umberto entertains us with his bowling app and Carly tries to teach Frank how to unscrew the top of the water bottle, a skill he'll have to master when he leaves for monkey college next year. Capuchin monkeys like Frank make great companions for people with disabilities; I don't want Frank to

overjoyed

downloaded

leave, but I know the person he'll end up living with will be overjoyed to have him.

My parents moved their cars down the street so the giant truck can pull into our driveway. Matt downloaded a ton of songs that will be perfect background music for having a party on a Monster Truck.

"How about if Frank and Bodi join us?" Umberto asks.

My mother says she wants us to have a fun day without worrying about taking care of animals, which is just another way of saying no.

We all run to the end of the driveway when we hear a giant truck pull down the street. I do a quick check over my shoulder to see if Steve is outside to witness this awesome spectacle.

A guy with a Dodgers hat jumps out of the truck and asks me where he should set up. I point to the driveway and he hops back in. My friends and I look on the back of the flatbed. Something large is onboard but it doesn't look like a Monster Truck. When the guy starts unloading onto the driveway, I ask him what's up.

He looks at me quizzically, then pulls an order form from his back pocket. "You ordered the Monster Truck bounce house, right?" As he talks, he starts to pump up the inflatable bouncer.

inflatable

"This is a Monster Truck BOUNCE HOUSE?" I yell. "I ordered a REAL Monster Truck!"

The man chuckles as the bouncer inflates. "Then I don't know why you called me. I rent bouncers for kids' parties."

Matt's in shock but Umberto bursts out laughing.

Carly just shakes her head. "You didn't finish reading, right? You saw the words 'Monster Truck' and just stopped there?"

It's scary how well Carly knows me.

"We had a whole conversation," I tell the man. "I thought we were talking about the TRUCK going up and down, not the bounce house!"

Carly puts on her most helpful face. "Well, let's make the best of it and have some fun."

But I don't want to have fun in a little kids' party bouncer. I want to hang off a giant truck with six-foot tires and a deafening engine. I want

deafening

photos I can blow up to poster size and hang in my room and locker.

Matt points to the bright red and yellow plastic truck now set up in my driveway. "Technically it IS a Monster Truck."

Umberto looks at the moon bounce that he couldn't use if he wanted to and tells me he's heading home. I ask the man if there's any way to make the bouncer handicap accessible but he says no. Umberto explains that it's no big deal, that he has to go home soon, but I know it's a total lie.

Matt kicks off his sneakers and somersaults into the moon bounce. "Come on in—the water's fine!"

somersaults

Carly joins him and soon they're having a contest to see who can jump the highest.

My father just shrugs while my mom slips her arm around me. I sneak out of her hug.

"It's not what you thought but it's still fun," Mom says. "I agree with Carly—make the best of it."

To my horror, Steve and his little brother are making their way across the yard. I mumble an introduction to my mom.

introduction

"Taylor was wondering if he could join in," Steve asks.

Taylor's already halfway into the bouncer, not waiting for an answer.

"It was supposed to be a REAL Monster Truck," I tell Steve.

He shrugs, then waits for my mother to leave. "By the way, my parents made me repaint the kitchen. Thanks a lot, loser." He sticks his earbuds in and heads back to his house. This is what I get for trying to impress a kid who's got zero interest in being my friend.

The guy from the rental company hands me forms on a clipboard to sign. "I hope you're not too disappointed," he says. "Most of our customers are usually happy with our service."

I'm barely listening because I'm too busy staring at the form. When you add up the rental fee, the taxes, and delivery, all the money I made from Baby Goldmine is now gone.

delivery

The man tears off the bottom sheet and hands it to me. "You've got another hour and a half—might as well start jumping."

I take his advice and climb into the bouncer. Jumping around IS pretty fun, until Matt accidentally lands on Taylor, who runs home crying, and Carly loses one of her tiny earrings that takes us twenty minutes to find. Not to mention Steve and several of his friends sitting on his front steps watching us, probably with a running commentary about how lame we are. By the time the bouncer is packed up, I'm not sure which of us is more deflated.

After Carly goes home, Matt and I sit on the back steps where he steals a look at the receipt and lets out a long whistle. "I feel like my dad, complaining about how expensive everything is," Matt says. "That cost a fortune!"

"Maybe we should've just had a grilled cheese party after all."

commentary

Matt scans the texts coming in on his phone, staring at the voice bubbles as if they're messages from the underworld.

underworld

"It's my brother. There's a problem with Baby Karen."

"Didn't the woman get the package?"

"She got it all right," Matt says. "But she wants her money back."

"What? That money's history."

"Yeah well, so are we if we don't take care of this."

"How can we pay her back? I just spent all the money!"

"All I know is my brother's furious. He wants to see us NOW."

This isn't how I thought my superfun and EXPENSIVE day would end.

The Other Shoe Drops

Matt and I pace around his kitchen, waiting for Jamie.

"The woman who bought the doll wrote Jamie a nasty e-mail," he says. "She said she's going to give him a bad eBay rating. He told me we have to take care of this pronto."

As if to emphasize the point, Jamie suddenly appears. "I make a lot of money selling my stuff online," he says. "And you two are putting my business in jeopardy."

jeopardy

I apologize ten times but Jamie's still hopping mad. "I let you guys use my log-in and password! My reputation is at stake. Your buyer's going to give me a bad review!"

reputation

I nod but can't help thinking how much trouble Jamie's gotten into in the past—not just when he was our age but recently too. To use one of my parents' favorite idioms, it's a case of "the pot calling the kettle black." But Jamie's so mad, there's no way I'm bringing that up now.

"You've got to return that woman's money." Jamie leans in close to Matt, who in turn leans toward me.

"Can I write her an e-mail?" I ask

meekly. "Maybe see if I can send her the money after Christmas?"

Jamie looks at me like I'm the biggest bunionhead he's ever met. And given some of Jamie's friends, that's saying something.

"Besides, why does she want her money back?" I ask. "What was wrong with Baby Karen?"

Jamie scrolls through the messages on his phone, until he finds the woman's e-mail. "'You said this doll was in excellent condition, which is why I paid so much money. But any collector knows Baby Karen comes with a black purse, which was not included, even though you said it was like new. I am returning your package today; please process a full refund immediately.'"

refund

"She's worried about the doll's

purse? SHE'S the one with the problem, not us!" I say.

Jamie grows even more annoyed. "If you say something is in perfect condition, it means it's like brand-new, with all the pieces! Don't you guys know anything?"

"I never saw a purse," Matt says. "Was it in the box?"

For the life of me, I cannot remember.

Jamie points to us both. "You two are sending her that refund or you'll have to deal with me AND her. You better pray she's not some hotshot attorney. She could take you to court."

attorney

I have no idea if that's true, but I've seen enough TV shows to know I don't want it to happen. When I picture myself on the witness stand

gavel

frightening

with a judge banging his gavel, I feel like I might start crying.

After Jamie leaves, Matt looks as concerned as I am. "You've got to take care of this! I haven't seen Jamie this mad since we scratched his car!"

Memories of that afternoon with our runaway scooters come flooding in, frightening me even more.

"You've got to tell your parents," Matt continues. "Borrow the money, give the refund, then pay them back."

"You know how long it'll take to pay back that much money? I'll be their slave for years. Plus, I wasn't the only one who enjoyed the day." I feel my fear slowly turning to anger. "Why should I be the only one to pay the woman back?"

"Because it was *your* party, your idea. You made us promise not to give you money!" Matt seems angry now too. "You just wanted your cool new neighbor to think you were a big shot. Well, newsflash—big shots pay."

newsflash

I jump on my board and head home, embarrassed that Matt figured out my secret motive with Steve. Was it that obvious?

As I race down the hill, my head bursts with all my mistakes. Why didn't I just keep Baby Goldmine with the other dolls? Why did I think I was some kind of super-businessman? Why did I spend all that money on a stupid moon bounce? Why did I think I could mail a doll to a total stranger and suddenly be rich? WHAT IS MY PROBLEM?

I tear apart the top shelf of my closet and look inside all of my sneakers for Baby Karen's purse. I look through the room we wrapped the package in; I even search Frank's cage. (He loves stealing my toys.) I rummage through the living room and kitchen but the purse is nowhere to be found. I'm not sure I ever had it in the first place.

It's obviously time to throw myself on the mercy of the court so I don't have to go to a real one. I take small comfort in Bodi, who slips underneath my chair, tail wagging. From his cage, Frank seems happy to see me too. I say the words I was hoping to say less and less this year:

"Mom? I need your help."

Another Teaching Moment

My mother listens patiently to my story, interrupting a few times to clarify the details. When I finally finish, she pauses before answering.

interrupting

"I thought you told us you won that money in a raffle."

I make my eyes as sad as they can be and stare back at her wordlessly.

clarify

"That's a pretty big lie, Derek."

The sorrowful expression is obviously not working. "I know," I admit. "That's why I'm in so much trouble now."

She wipes the cornbread crumbs off the kitchen table. "Well, if you *were* going to keep one of the donations and sell it, you probably should've done some research to see if the doll came with accessories."

accessories

"I've never been good with research. You KNOW that."

My mom listens calmly. Maybe this won't be as bad as I thought.

"I guess looking back, you might have left that doll with the others. Someone donated her to the shelter, not to you."

I tell my mom I know that and as soon as the buyer sends the doll back, I'm taking it straight to the shelter.

"I think that's smart." She throws the handful of crumbs into the trash.

"So..." I let the rest of the sentence hang in the air, waiting for her to lend me the money so I can pay back the buyer immediately before Jamie comes after me.

"Well, I'm glad you finally told me the truth," Mom says.

"And?" I gather up my mental strength to finish the conversation. "If I could just borrow the money to pay her back, that would be great."

My mother seems perplexed. "You want me to lend you money after you lied to my face?"

perplexed

Why did I think she'd forget that tiny detail of the story? "It

steadfast

would just be a loan. I'd pay you back after Christmas and my birthday."

She doesn't seem angry, just steadfast. "I thought you wanted to be a big kid this year—more responsible and mature?"

I tell her that's true.

"Well, if you want to be treated more like a grown-up, you can't have your mom bail you out. You'll have to figure a way to fix this yourself."

"But I DID figure a way out— getting money from you."

"That wouldn't be learning much of a lesson, would it? Especially for a serious crime like lying."

"This isn't about learning a lesson! Besides, lying isn't a CRIME." After the sentence leaves my mouth, it dawns on me that lying probably

CAN be a crime. But not this time. "Come on! Jamie's going to kill me!"

"You're the one with all these schemes. I'm sure you'll figure out a great way to solve your problem." She loads the dishwasher as if the conversation's over.

"Mom! This isn't the time to start being hands-off! I need you to be hands-on and help me!"

She shoves some utensils into the tray. "I *am* helping you—to pay the consequences of your actions. I have total faith you'll come up with a good solution."

I have one thought and one thought only—to get to my father before Mom does. As I jump over Bodi to head upstairs, my mother calls over her shoulder, "Your father had a ceremony to go

ceremony

to with some work friends. I'll be sure to fill him in on all this before he gets home."

Dad's always been a softer touch than Mom. Why didn't I go to him first? I scold myself for not planning this out better and head up to my room.

What am I going to do NOW?

A Different Plan

Because my mother's using this giant fiasco as a learning experience, it feels like she threw me into the deep end of a pool before teaching me to swim. How am I supposed to come up with that much money in just a few days when I've never earned more than a few dollars in my whole life?

I rack my brain trying to come

measly

up with ways to raise money that won't get me into as much trouble as my last plan did. Robbing a bank is out, as is raiding my own savings, which totals a measly twenty-one dollars. I make a list of the lamest, stupidest ideas on the planet, then do what I always do when I need a bigger brain than my own—call Carly.

It goes without saying that Carly is NOT pleased when I admit to the Baby Goldmine scheme. (She believed the raffle story too.) But by the end of my confession, she almost feels sorry for me.

confession

"Too bad you can't just rewind back to the day you took the doll," she says.

Hanging out with us has obviously rubbed off on Carly; this suggestion is something Matt would come up with. "It's not like I STOLE the doll. Somebody gave her away."

"To the shelter—not to you."

"Come on, you're my friend! My friend who always knows what to do."

"I'm also the friend who was there when you made your New Year's resolution. You wanted to be more mature. Well, here's your chance."

Talk about rewinding to a certain moment—I wish I could rewind to New Year's Day and take back that stupid resolution. I beg and plead but Carly remains as unwavering as my mom.

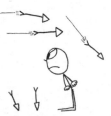

unwavering

So after school I implement the first item on my list of money-making ideas: a car wash. Schools

lure

always do car washes to raise funds—it's a good plan.

Matt and Umberto help me lure customers into the Home Depot parking lot near our house. (I don't think the skinny manager who said we could use the corner of the lot was paying attention when he said yes.) Even with Umberto racing around with a giant sign that says CAR WASH on his lap, we get only three customers. The last one complains we don't do a good job and makes us wash her minivan twice. We end up making twelve dollars, which would usually be good news. Not today.

minivan

"It was too short notice," Matt says.

"Oh, NOW you've got advice?" I answer.

"School car washes are always in the newsletters and on the website a few weeks before."

"Besides," Umberto adds, "this isn't for school. It's more like a 'Help Save Our Friend's Butt' car wash."

I pull the folded list from my pocket and scan my options. "Make Frank wear a little jacket and bow tie, begging for money while I play the accordion?"

accordion

"You don't play the accordion," Matt and Umberto say together.

"I know, but wouldn't it be great to see Frank in one of those little suits, carrying a tiny cup?"

"What else have you got?" Umberto snatches away my list. "A golf tournament? You probably need months to plan something like that."

Matt looks over Umberto's

shoulder. "Sell frozen cookie dough? What are you, a chef now?"

"You know how many truckloads of cookie dough you'd have to sell door-to-door to make two hundred thirty-two dollars?" Umberto asks.

Now it's my turn to snatch the list away. "You guys are a lot of help."

"Hey! We washed cars with frozen hands all afternoon," Matt says. "You can't complain."

asphalt

I empty the bucket of dirty water onto the asphalt, turn it over, and take a seat. "Jamie's going to kill me."

Matt asks if I tried asking my dad for the money.

"My mom's hiding him. It's like he's in the witness protection program. I haven't seen him in two days."

As we wait for our parents to pick us up, we wander the aisles of Home Depot, pretending to hit ourselves in the head with hammers, then fall on the floor like cartoon characters. The skinny manager watches us without yelling but without laughing either.

inquires

"How'd it go?" my mom inquires on the drive home.

"I'm surprised you care," I answer. "Since you're the one who wants me to fail."

"No. I'm the one who wants you to *learn*." She thankfully focuses on the traffic instead of me.

She talks about the Siamese cat she's treating for a skin disease and how Mrs. Mitchell is having second thoughts about moving. I know she hates it when I use my phone while someone else is talking, so I sneak my cell near the door handle to read the new text from Matt.

Doll here. Jamie home tmrw. U R dead meat.

express

The buyer must've used an express mail service to get Baby Not-Such-a-Goldmine here so fast. I know Jamie and his girlfriend are in Santa Barbara, which is only two hours away.

My time is just about up.

Baby Disaster

When I try to bum a piece of candy from Carly before class the next morning, she quietly slides a notebook under her math textbook. It's a small spiral pad, the kind reporters use on TV shows. I ask her why she's hiding it.

swipe

She says she isn't, which just makes me swipe it from her desk. "Is it a diary?" I ask. "Notes to a secret crush?"

But the book is filled with dates and titles of novels borrowed from the library. "Are these all the books you've read this year?" The list is longer than the list of books I've read in my entire life. "There are so many!"

She shrugs as if it's no big deal.

achievement

"Why are you hiding it?" I ask. "It's an achievement—you should show it off." It dawns on me why she's hiding the notebook. "You're worried I'll feel bad about being such a crummy reader. That I could never in a million years read a book a week—unless they were baby books."

She doesn't look me in the eye when she answers. "That's not true."

But I know it is.

I sit at the empty desk beside

her. "Or is it because you kept your New Year's resolution and I didn't keep mine?"

Carly steals the notebook back. "I wasn't hiding this. I was just putting it away." She looks down, suddenly captivated by the inside cover of her math book.

captivated

I shuffle back to my desk feeling more like a joke than I usually do. There's no way around the fact that school is getting harder with each month that goes by. Even though I stumbled through elementary school, that was nothing compared to the amount of work I have to do now. Kids like Carly and Maria and Umberto might be able to sail through homework in two seconds, but this year I've had to dedicate more time just to keep up. Not to

stumbled

dedicate

mention the muscles I've built up lugging around my four-thousand-pound book bag. What's going to happen next year and the year after that? Will my every waking moment be spent trying to keep my head above water?

I look over at Carly, now engrossed in the paperback she keeps tucked in her bag, and feel a stab of envy. I think about New Year's Day when she made that vow and how she had the discipline to stick with it, not try and find a shortcut like I did. I think about all the people who glued lentils and marigolds onto those Rose Bowl floats—they had goals they achieved too. I'd love to be patient and focused, but as much as I try to be, I never end up with the same results as someone like Carly.

Of course, it doesn't help that I fall asleep during history class later that afternoon. It was only for a few minutes but it was enough time to have a dream of Jamie driving a golf cart and chasing me as I race across the course. He was steering the cart with one hand and whacking golf balls at me with the other. I wake up with a start and almost fall out of my chair. Matt laughs but when he gets a look at my panicked face, he realizes it isn't funny.

panicked

"Are you worried about my brother?" he asks on the way home. "Because you *should* be. I swear he'll drive us both up to the canyon and leave us there till we get attacked by mountain lions or scorched in a wildfire."

scorched

"If you're going to throw in every

natural disaster known to man, don't forget earthquakes and mudslides," I say.

"And monsoons," Matt adds.

"And tsunamis."

"And tornadoes."

Our disaster routine takes my mind off my troubles for a few minutes, but not enough. After going on way too long, Matt checks his phone. "Jamie will be home in a few hours. Are you ready to face the music?"

"If by music you mean him playing the cymbals on either side of my head, then no." I tell Matt I have one last idea to try. Seeing Carly's reading list today motivated me to be as smart as I can be. My last plan is unpredictable but worth trying. If Carly can stick with her resolution, maybe I can too.

motivated

unpredictable

A Last Resort

I made a list of all the people who could possibly help me: Grammy, Mrs. Mitchell, maybe even Ms. McCoddle. But deep down I knew there was a little bit of truth to Mom's notion of me fixing this myself. Sure, borrowing money from Grammy would have been a slam dunk, but when I made that vow to try to be more grown up

destiny

this year, I really meant it. (Besides, a check from Boston probably would not get here in time.) So I ride my bike across town to decide my destiny.

I salute Mrs. Sweeney on the way into my old elementary school. She salutes back without straying from her huge stack of papers.

I hurry down the hall and wait outside the cafeteria where the smell of freshly baked brownies makes me hungry.

"Excuse me, Ms. McManus." In my eagerness I almost knock over the woman with the high heels and the metallic blue fingernails.

She has to balance herself not to fall. "Derek, right? How are you doing?" She suddenly looks terrified. "Did I miss a meeting?"

"No, I called your office and they

said you were here today. I was wondering if we could talk."

She checks her phone for the time, then hands me a box of flyers. "Let's talk in here." She leads me to a table in the back of the cafeteria.

"Let me guess," she says. "You had such a good time volunteering, you want to sign up for more? We get that a lot."

"Not exactly." I take a deep breath and launch into the saga of Baby Goldmine.

saga

At the end of my tale of woe, she tilts her head and looks me over. "I'm wondering why you're telling me all this."

"You seem really busy, and I wanted to see if you needed an assistant, someone to help you carry stuff to your car, hand out flyers, that kind of thing."

She buzzes through texts on her phone as she listens to me. "I suppose you want an advance, right? To make your little doll problem go away?"

I tell her an advance of two hundred thirty-two dollars would be a lifesaver.

"My assistant is on maternity leave and I'm very behind, so here's the deal." She puts down her phone. "First, we call your mother to make sure it's okay. If it is, you can be my assistant for the next month. I've got several fund-raisers planned—you'll have to get a ride to the meetings."

Even though my mom wouldn't lend me the money, she's never complained about chauffeuring me around town for appointments. I tell

chauffeuring

Ms. McManus transportation won't be a problem.

transportation

Ms. McManus grabs her wallet and counts out a pile of twenties. I'm not sure, but I don't think either of my parents carries around this much money on a normal day. Just as she's about to hand it to me, she pulls back and tells me to get my mother on the phone. As she talks to Mom on my cell, I can't help but stare at the money that's in Ms. McManus's hand. Really, who carries around all that cash?

"Your mom says it's okay if you work for me, so here you go." She hands me the money that will repay my debt. "I'll see you tomorrow at six at the Hammer Museum. Do you know where that is?"

debt

I tell her yes but don't tell her it's

because I got dragged there on a
field trip last year.

"You're earning the money fair
and square; your parents should be
proud."

Proud isn't a word that comes to
mind when I think about this whole
Baby Goldmine disaster. I can't help
asking Ms. McManus why she trusts
me. "How do you know I won't just
take off with this money and never
pay you back?"

She looks at me as if she never
even considered the possibility. "I
don't know." She shrugs. "I just
assume you're a man of your word."

assume

There's that word again—*man.*

"Besides," she says, "I have all
your info—I know where you live."
She stands up and stares at the
giant box on the table.

I realize my assistant duties begin immediately and carry the box to her car.

"By the way," she says as she closes the trunk, "call me Debbie."

As I ride home on my bike, I think about how funny things turn out sometimes. How a stranger you didn't like is the person who ends up helping you when you need it. Like one of those stories where a random person donates a kidney to some guy in need of a transplant, THAT'S how much Ms. McManus— I mean, Debbie—helped me out today.

transplant

I tried to be a cool money-making superhero but wound up as someone's sidekick instead. There are worse things—namely, being at the other end of Jamie's fist.

I Am Now a
Worker Bee

I give the money to Jamie, who
immediately sends the refund to the
buyer in order to save his precious
rating. He doesn't smile or act happy
that I got the money back; instead
he's all business. As soon as we're
done, I can tell he wants me to leave,
so I do.

My mom drives me to my first
day of work at my new job. She

comes inside the Hammer Museum to meet Debbie, whom she's only spoken to on the phone. Mom apologizes for the whole Baby Karen thing—even though it's my fault, not hers—but Debbie says she's happy to have the help.

"It may take a while for you to earn that money back," my mom tells me before she leaves. "But you used your resources and solved your own problem. Plus you're learning new skills and working in the community—all good things."

And it WAS good, at least that first day. The second day was okay too. And the third. But by the end of the first week of helping out after school, I have to admit I was exhausted. I couldn't believe how many different jobs were involved in putting an event together. Compiling lists of donors, printing name badges, doing seating charts, making phone calls, looking up stuff on the computer—my afternoons and weekends were full of ... what's the word? Oh yeah, WORK.

The jobs weren't the only things that were different—so were the locations. During the next several weeks, I met Debbie and her volunteers at the women's shelter downtown, the YMCA in Santa Monica, the Wildlife Rescue Center in Culver City, and the Observatory at Griffith Park. I thought I'd been to most places in L.A. but it turns out I'd never seen lots of cool features of the city. As much as it was a month of labor, parts of it were fun too.

observatory

Today we're setting up a fund-raiser for Big Brother/Big Sister and Debbie asks me to organize a giant pile of name tags into alphabetical order on the table by the door. Like most afternoons of working with her, I'm too busy to check the clock once. Filling gift bags, rearranging chairs, putting out literature—I can barely take a bathroom break before it's time to go home.

ANDERSON
BUTTONS
CARREY
DANIELS
EDWARDS

alphabetical

Debbie looks around the room approvingly. "We're going to have a nice event here tonight, Derek. You and the other volunteers have done a great job."

approvingly

I glance at the others helping get the room ready for tonight's event. "Is everyone working for free?"

"Of course they are," Debbie

answers. "This is a fund-raiser—everyone's volunteering."

"But... you paid me."

She takes a stack of pamphlets and fans them out in a different pattern than I had them. "You needed a break and I'm in the business of helping people. It wasn't a tough decision."

slack-jawed

I stare at her slack-jawed until she bursts out laughing.

"I needed help, you needed to make money—it's not brain surgery." She reaches into her giant bag as if she just remembered something. "Speaking of brain surgery, can you meet me at the Central Library downtown Friday afternoon? There's a brain-injury awareness program and I need some escort help."

Dragging a bunch of old fogies

around a library on a Friday afternoon sounds like the worst event
EVER, but Debbie's given me a new
perspective on helping people out. I
tell her no problem.

perspective

She hands me a brochure from
her bag. "There'll be a Q-and-A panel
with some press afterward. It'll just
be a few hours."

I stare at the brochure in my
hand. "Tony Hawk's going to be
there?"

"You know him? He's doing a
demonstration on helmets and
brain injury. He's the person you'll
escort. You skateboard, right?"

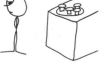

willpower

It takes every bit of willpower
not to race down the stairs,
screaming at the top of my lungs.
I'll be with TONY HAWK? If Matt
has to invent a secret shrinking potion

translate

so he can fit in my pocket, he'll find a way to come too.

I don't need my mom to translate this into a teaching moment: If this is what happens when you help people out, count me in.

Matt Goes Crazy

As expected, Matt insists on coming with me Friday afternoon. "I can sweep up, pass out flyers—I'll even hold Tony's gum while he talks if you want me to."

Then I tell Matt the best part of the news—that Debbie already told me it was okay for him to come.

Matt literally starts screaming.

When he finally winds down, he unzips his pack and hands me a package. I don't need to ask what it is as I unwrap it.

"I want to run this doll over with my bike," I say.

"Stupid doll—losing her purse. How were we supposed to know?"

It's hard to blame a lump of plastic

misplaced

for losing one of her accessories when it was probably some little kid like Olivia who misplaced it years ago, the same way I've misplaced toys a million times. I take a minute

handmade

to finally look at the doll. She's got long black hair and thick eyelashes; she looks old-fashioned but well cared for. Her little red coat and dress look handmade. I guess if you were a girl who had to play with a doll, you could make a worse choice than Baby Karen.

"You should resell her," Matt says. "Just tell people she doesn't have the purse."

"As if Jamie's ever going to let us use his account again."

"You're right. Jamie is never helping us do ANYTHING again."

Matt wants us to practice some of our skateboard moves to show Tony tomorrow but I tell him the day's going to be all work.

"Yeah, but the GOOD kind of work." Matt is kicking the grass with nervous excitement when Mrs. Mitchell's daughter comes over and asks if she can talk to me.

"I'm wondering if I might bother you to babysit for a few hours today," Mandy asks.

The spirit of meeting Tony Hawk must still be hovering over me because I tell her okay.

hovering

She looks down to where Matt has made a mess of the lawn. "Babysitting is the wrong word," Mandy says. "It's my mother I want you to stay with, not Olivia."

I ask if Mrs. Mitchell is sick. The question seems to make Mandy sad.

"She's been wandering around the neighborhood lately," Mandy says. "Yesterday she ended up at the pharmacy and didn't remember how she got there. I'll worry about her much less when she comes to live with me."

I've got some homework for history class due tomorrow—maybe Mrs. Mitchell can help me with it while I'm there. I tell Mandy I'll be right over.

"You're going to babysit an

pharmacy

eighty-year-old?" Matt asks. "I'd rather stick toothpicks in my eyes."

I tell him there are worse things than hanging out with Mrs. Mitchell, not to mention the fact that she's the best baker I know.

Unfortunately, when I get to her house, there are no warm goodies from the oven, just Mrs. Mitchell sitting in her chair gazing out the window. "Everything's getting ready to bloom," she says. "You can see the buds on the cherry tree. Any day now the sky will be full of blossoms."

admiring

Admiring trees is definitely less fun than eating warm cupcakes but I settle into the chair next to Mrs. Mitchell. We play cards until Mandy gets back from her errands. It's a

slow way to spend an afternoon but
two words make me not even THINK
about complaining.

TONY HAWK!

The Big Event

Matt and I arrive at the Central Library half an hour early—a first for us. As someone who's been pretty much allergic to books my whole life, I have to admit that the library building is impressive—it's gigantic and old with a huge mural depicting the history of California. Matt and I ride the escalators up and down, trying to ease our nerves.

depicting

"Suppose he doesn't show up?" Matt asks.

I don't have to ask who he's talking about; Tony Hawk is all we've discussed for days. "He's on all the advertising," I reassure him. "He'll be here."

advertising

Matt's usually so easygoing that it's funny to see him this anxious. I introduce him to Debbie, who puts the two of us to work, helping out two grown-up volunteers. It's our job to make sure each table has information packets for the people attending the fund-raiser to take home.

I reach into my pack and hand Baby Karen to Debbie.

"Is this what started your whole mess?" she asks.

When I tell her I think the doll

might be cursed, Debbie laughs. "If
that's the case, you can't give her
back to the children's shelter. The
kids there don't need an evil doll—
they have enough problems."

cursed

I try to decide if she's pulling my
leg.

"The shelter project is done,"
Debbie says. "And we have our
hands full today. The doll's all yours."
She barks out an order to open the
doors, and people start filing in.

I shove the doll back into my pack
and get to work. After a while, the
news spreads upstairs that Tony
Hawk has arrived. Matt looks like he
might collapse with the prospect of
meeting him.

But before our skateboard idol
comes upstairs, I spot Steve from
next door in the crowd. He seems

infamous

as shocked to see me as I am to see him. He's accompanied by several of his friends from the infamous party.

"What are YOU doing here?" I realize after I ask him that my question probably sounds rude.

But Steve answers anyway. "My mom's a big believer in helmet safety, so she got tickets. And when I found out that Tony Hawk was going to be here, I begged her to let me come instead." He gestures to his friends. "Turns out everyone wanted to see him, so my mom's company bought a whole table." He looks at the name tag I'm wearing. "What are YOU doing here?"

I shrug as if it's no big deal, which of course is a giant lie. "I'm Tony's escort. It's my job to make sure he knows where he's supposed to be while he's here." I gesture over to Matt now standing protectively behind me. "OUR job."

protectively

Steve can't hide the fact that he's awestruck by this news. "You're in charge of TONY HAWK?"

awestruck

What I want to say is "Yes, maybe you shouldn't have treated me like such a loser that night." Instead I just shrug. Matt smiles as if hanging out with a skateboard god is a normal event for us.

I don't have time to bask in the envy of Steve and his friends—we have work to do. Matt and I usher people to their tables, hand out information, and wait for Mike, the head volunteer, to text us when it's time to take Tony to the press room. When I look over at Steve, he still looks stunned.

disguise

distraught

My phone buzzes and I tell Matt we're on. But the text isn't from Mike downstairs; it's an emergency text from my mother. I hide myself in a corner of the room and call her back.

She can't disguise the panic in her voice. "Mrs. Mitchell's gone. Mandy's distraught. We've looked all over the neighborhood but can't find her." She lowers her voice. "I know you've got a big day there. I just wanted to see if you had any ideas where she might be."

I ask my mother if they checked the pharmacy where Mandy found her a few weeks ago. "She's not in the village," my mom says. "I just wanted to check in. You have fun and we'll see you when you get home."

The flash of cameras and din of reporters make their way upstairs and I tell my mom to hold on. Matt holds his phone up with the text from Mike: It's time for us to get Tony Hawk.

din

"Is Dad still downtown?" I ask my mom. "I know he was going to the art supply store after he dropped us off."

She tells me my father is downtown now but getting on the highway to come home and look for Mrs. Mitchell.

"Tell him to pick me up."

My mother's voice is calm and caring. "You stay there and enjoy your time with Tony Hawk. We've got this covered."

"Tell Dad I'll be waiting outside the library." When I end the call,

Matt looks like he's about to go into shock.

"You can't leave!" Matt says. "We're in charge of Tony Hawk!"

I tell my best friend I have to go and hurry through the room to find Debbie. She must be able to tell from the look on my face that what I have to say is important.

"Is everything okay?" She greets people at the door as she talks to me.

"No," I answer. "My neighbor's missing."

feathered

She turns away from a woman in a giant feathered hat and bends down to my height. "Do you need someone to drive you?"

I tell her my father's on his way.

"Let me know if there's anything I can do." I want to thank her but she's back at work, greeting the next attendee.

I race down the escalator and out into the street—just in time to see the top of Tony Hawk's head.

attendee

A-HA!

energizing

Outside the library, they're filming something that looks like a car commercial because about twenty sedans of the same make and model keep driving by, then backing up again down the street. I watch the policemen direct traffic around the truck with the cameras, but as energizing as it always is to see things filmed on the streets of L.A., all I can think about now is Mrs. Mitchell.

I've been complaining about Mrs. Mitchell moving to Calabasas with her daughter but now I understand why Mandy wants to have her close by. There's nothing funny about being lost in a city this size.

I stand on my toes to see if I can spot my dad's car coming down the street.

All year I've been trying to act older than I am, pretending I'm grown-up instead of the goofy twelve-year-old I really am. Mrs. Mitchell has the opposite problem— fighting age from the other side. I bet she'd give anything to be younger, even if it meant being immature again.

opposite

I sneak back inside the library to

get a glimpse of Matt and our hero but can't see past the crowd looking for their name tags on the reception table. By now, Matt's probably walking down those long hallways talking secret skateboard techniques with Tony Hawk. I'm jealous but not enough to change where I'm headed.

I stand on the top library step and watch the truck with the cameras take yet another pass down the street. The sedans drive toward the intersection, then slowly back up the hill for the next take. It reminds me of when I was a stuntboy in a teen movie, doing take after take on my board until I got it right. This director certainly has a great day for filming; the sky is a perfect blue and the pink

intersection

blossoms are falling from the trees like bits of cotton candy.

In an instant, my mind snaps into focus and I know exactly where to find Mrs. Mitchell. I text my father the address, then break into a run.

Hope and Flower

canopy

inescapable

This time of year, the city explodes with pink bursts from all the jacaranda trees but some streets are more colorful than others. As I hurry down Flower Street from the library, I see what Mrs. Mitchell was talking about. Where the street turns into Hope, the canopy of color is inescapable. I stop running to catch my breath and soak in all that pink.

As I look down the aisles of trees, I'm happy to see my hunch was correct. Mrs. Mitchell is sitting on one of the benches, staring up at the sky. I slide beside her without saying a word.

A huge smile crosses her face when she sees me. "I told you this was the best spot in the city."

I tell her she was right, then ask her how she got here.

"The bus," she answers, not knowing there's a posse back home looking for her. "I always take the bus." After a moment she looks over at me as if seeing me for the first time. "You seem like a nice young man."

posse

I quickly realize Mrs. Mitchell doesn't know who I am. A wave of panic rushes over me—not because

Mrs. Mitchell doesn't recognize me but because I'm the only one in charge of her safety right now. The panic turns to terror. What if something happens and I don't know what to do?

She looks down the street at the rows of trees. "I like that one best." Mrs. Mitchell points to the tree closest to us. I tell her I like that one too.

I've never been so relieved to see my dad as he approaches from the other side of the street.

Mrs. Mitchell watches my dad come toward us. "Walter! The trees are amazing this year, aren't they?"

My father's name is Jeremy; Walter was Mr. Mitchell, who died last year. But my dad doesn't correct her, just takes a seat. "I

relieved

think it's the best year for jacarandas I've ever seen."

I wait for him to lead her to the car but he doesn't. He quietly sends a text—probably to my mom telling her we found Mrs. Mitchell— then continues looking up at the trees.

After a while, Mrs. Mitchell turns to my father with a start. "Jeremy! What a surprise!" She tousles my hair. "You've got quite a kid here—a boy who appreciates nature."

appreciates

"He IS quite a kid," Dad agrees. "A kid whose quick thinking saved the day."

This is the first time in my life where my thinking's been labeled "quick," so I let the word sink in. QUICK THINKING—me!

Dad extends his arm for Mrs. Mitchell to hold on to and we head toward the car. "Derek, aren't you due back at the library?" he asks.

My parents have been trying to get me to libraries my entire life. I guess the missing ingredient was that Tony Hawk was never there.

"You're a hero," Dad whispers to me as we walk. "I'll take Mrs. Mitchell; you go home with Matt the way we planned."

The event's probably half over by now but I don't complain. Even escorting Tony Hawk around can't compare with saving the day in your neighborhood. After helping Mrs. Mitchell into Dad's car, I look down the street where Flower Street turns to Hope. It IS beautiful; I can understand why Mrs. Mitchell tried so hard to get here.

But now it's time to race back to the library.

Did I just say that?

Better Late
Than Never

lecture

Turns out that I only missed a boring lecture from a UCLA doctor and a slideshow on their new medical center. I sneak into the auditorium just as Tony Hawk's about to take the stage.

Tony talks about the importance of skateboard safety and states several statistics about how important it is to wear a properly fitted helmet. While all the attendees look on, he conducts a mini clinic, talking not only about helmets but elbow- and kneepads. Matt and I wear our helmets faithfully, but I have to admit, sometimes we do skate without our pads. Matt sidles over to me while Tony talks.

faithfully

"He shook my hand," Matt whispers. "And signed my shirt!" He pulls out a blue T-shirt from one of the gift bags. Sure enough— Tony Hawk's signature is scrawled underneath the logo.

scrawled

I tell Matt the gift bags aren't for us, but he says Debbie told him it was okay to take one. He smiles and holds up another autographed shirt for me. Of COURSE my best friend didn't forget about me.

autographed

"Is everything okay?" Debbie whispers.

I tell her about Mrs. Mitchell and

explain that she's on her way back home.

Debbie looks at me a few moments before responding. "I was at the school committee meeting when your principal brought up mandatory community service. No matter what the committee decides, I think your school's already found a great volunteer."

I must look unnerved because she laughs. "I'm not saying you should volunteer for everything that comes up. I just think you're good at it, that's all."

unnerved

The room breaks into applause, not for me but for Tony Hawk. I'm glad Debbie appreciates how hard I've worked.

"I'd love it if you'd continue volunteering," Debbie says. "But as of today, consider your debt paid off."

I feel the curse of Baby Goldmine suddenly lift and thank Debbie again for helping me out.

Matt says his mother's at the gelato place down the street and can drive us home whenever we're ready. Our last job is to hand out the gift bags and then we're free to go.

gelato

"Derek, one more thing." Debbie leads me over to the front of the room. "You have to meet our guest of honor."

I nearly collapse with a weird combination of joy and fear when she introduces me to Tony Hawk, who shakes my hand and thanks me for helping out today. Debbie whispers into his ear while I stumble out a hello.

"Hey, Derek, can I borrow your cell?" Tony asks.

I look left; I look right. Is he talking to ME?

I rummage through my pants pockets and hand him my cell.

"This is the same one I have," Tony says.

Matt and I stare at each other with senseless grins. TONY HAWK IS HOLDING MY PHONE.

senseless

Tony quickly hits the buttons for phone, voicemail, and record, then holds the phone up to his mouth. Is he changing my voicemail message?

"Hey, this is Tony Hawk. I'm out boarding with my buddy Derek. Leave your name and number and he'll get back to you as soon as he's done leaving me in the dust. Ciao!" He fist-bumps me, then tosses back the phone, which I am eternally grateful that I catch. Matt looks like he's about to pass out.

Tony gives us both a wave and heads into the throng of people waiting for him outside the door. As she guides him through the crowd, Debbie looks back at me and smiles.

throng

"You can never, ever change that message—you know that, right?" Matt says as we leave.

I stare at the phone in my hand as if it's the Holy Grail. "Maybe we've been missing out on this whole volunteering thing."

"You're just saying that 'cause Tony Hawk's on your voicemail forever." Matt dials my phone and leaves a message just to hear our idol's voice one more time.

I listen and laugh at Tony's

incentive

message too, but can't stop thinking about what Debbie said. I know there'll be other opportunities down the line where I WILL help her out, with or without the incentive of a skateboard god.

Who knows—maybe I ended up keeping my New Year's resolution after all.

A Neighbor Leaves

My mother gives me the longest, tightest hug when I get home and thanks me again for helping to find Mrs. Mitchell. I tell her it's no big deal, but considering that no one else thought Mrs. Mitchell might take a bus all the way downtown, maybe it IS a big deal. Mom says Mandy wants to thank me personally, so I tell her I'll go over after dinner.

Mrs. Mitchell taking off on her own makes me think twice about disregarding Mom's orders and letting Frank loose outside. Never mind how much trouble I'd get into with the foster monkey organization if he never came back—I'd MISS him. I always assumed if Frank took off, he'd just return on his own, but suppose he climbed through the trees and couldn't find his way? While Mom heats up beef and cauliflower stew, I lie on the living room rug with both my animal friends, glad they're safe and sound.

When I head over to Mrs. Mitchell's later, my never-miss-a-trick mom asks what's in the bag I'm carrying. I tell her it's a going-away present, which is true.

cauliflower

On my way to the Mitchells', I hear a noise coming up behind me; it's Steve on his board. He careens down the street, skidding to a stop in front of me, and tells me yet again how cool it was that I got to meet Tony Hawk. I just nod and let him talk. Even though my phone's in my pocket, I don't tell him about Tony's message.

careens

"Hey, I'm having some friends over tonight," Steve continues. "Why don't you come by?" He looks down at the ground, suddenly mesmerized by the manhole cover. "You don't have to watch my brother. Just come and hang."

mesmerized

I tell Steve thanks but I've got something to do and will see him around. It may be too soon to say—and I may take this back tomorrow—but for right now, impressing other people seems a lot less important than it used to.

Mandy greets me at the door like I'm her long-lost son, going on and on about how I saved the day. During Mandy's fuss, Mrs. Mitchell calmly takes a tray out of the oven as if the whole ordeal was a distant memory. I listen to Mandy talk about how great I am while the smell of warm oatmeal cookies with walnuts and chocolate chips fills the room. Compliments AND warm cookies? I may stay here forever.

It takes all my willpower to wait until Mrs. Mitchell puts the cookies on a plate before I grab one. After my third cookie, I take out the present I brought over.

Mrs. Mitchell's face lights up

distant

when she sees the doll. "Mandy, look! It's Baby Karen! I got her at that department store for your birthday!" Mrs. Mitchell combs the doll's hair with her fingers. "But where is her purse?"

Mrs. Mitchell has just asked the Two-Hundred-Thirty-Two-Dollar Question. I tell her I don't know.

"I have one!" Olivia runs into one of the bedrooms and comes out holding a little black bag.

"There it is!" Mrs. Mitchell says.

I stare at Olivia holding the now-complete Baby Karen. SHE had the purse this whole time?! She must've taken it that day when I tried to get her to play with the doll at my house. I feel myself get angry at all the trouble Olivia caused, then take a deep breath. I guess if Olivia hadn't taken the purse to play with, I wouldn't have had to return Baby Karen, which means I wouldn't have owed the money to that lady and wouldn't have worked with Debbie, which means I wouldn't have Tony Hawk on my outgoing phone message. (I've already called myself twenty times from other people's phones.) I exhale and watch Mrs. Mitchell with the doll.

absorbed

Mandy puts her arm on mine, happy to see her mother so absorbed with this favorite childhood toy.

"Come see the doll, Mandy," Mrs. Mitchell calls.

addressing

Mandy starts to walk across the room until we both realize Mrs. Mitchell is addressing Olivia. She holds up the doll to the toddler. "Mandy, Baby Karen's here."

Olivia just stares at her grand-mother blankly.

Seeing Mandy's face fall as she watches Mrs. Mitchell makes my heart ache. Mandy stays back with me, observing her mother and her daughter and her childhood doll.

I've tried to give Baby Karen to Olivia several times though she didn't want anything to do with her. But I guess even a toddler knows when it's time to think about someone else because Olivia thanks her grandmother and hugs the doll to her chest like Baby Karen is the greatest present in the world. Mandy looks happy and sad at the same time, which I didn't think was possible. It's like the doll has linked all of them through decades and I suddenly wonder if Baby Karen is cursed in a

GOOD way. Maybe my taking her out of the donation box wasn't such a bad thing after all. Maybe I DON'T have to grow up so soon. Maybe just being me—the goofy joke that I am—is all I have to do right now.

I grab Olivia's T. rex action figure from the box in the corner of the room and move it across the floor toward the couch, making loud, bellowing noises. Olivia lets out a pretend scream.

bellowing

"Uh-oh," Mandy says. "T. rex is coming for Baby Karen."

"No," I growl. "He's coming for Baby Karen's purse!"

Olivia shrieks with delight, then hides the doll under a stack of pillows, which of course the dinosaur demolishes. Mrs. Mitchell claps her hands and laughs as I make the dinosaur chase Olivia and the doll around the room. It's a Friday night and I'm on the floor playing with a little kid, a doll, and a dinosaur. I can't tell if that's mature or immature but I'm having too much fun to care.

Sometimes It's Okay to Be the Punchline

inane

A week later, Matt texts that he's on his way over. I assume we're going to laugh at people doing inane tricks on YouTube, but when I open the back door, I'm surprised to see he's with Umberto and Carly. They all look at my father awkwardly until Dad stands up and claps his hands.

"Get your stuff," Dad tells me. "We're going out."

I ask more than once where we're going but Dad's answer is inaudible, and even though I beg him to repeat himself, he doesn't. The same goes for Matt, Carly, and Umberto. Bill, who drives Umberto's van, has been to our house a lot but this time, he and my father exchange keys. It appears my father's taking my friends and me somewhere in the van while Bill uses my father's car. I can't say for sure because NO ONE'S TELLING ME ANYTHING.

inaudible

exchange

As we head east on the 10, I start guessing. "Are we going to the Wax Museum? That great frozen yogurt place in West Hollywood?" With each wrong guess, everyone's grin grows wider.

"What do you think?" Matt finally asks my dad. "Should we tell him?"

My dad says okay and Carly—of course—takes the lead. "This has been a rough year for you," she says.

"And it's only May!" Umberto adds.

"But it looks like things might be turning around." Matt holds up five tickets. "Which is why you need to see some REAL Monster Trucks."

I grab the tickets from his hand. Sure enough, they're for the big Monster Truck show at the Staples Center this afternoon.

"Dad, these cost a fortune!"

"They did, but I wasn't the one who paid. Mrs. Mitchell wanted to do something special for you and your friends as her going-away present. When I asked Matt, he suggested this. I told her I'd pay for you kids but Mrs. Mitchell insisted on treating all of us."

insisted

It seems like an unfair trade—I give Mrs. Mitchell a forty-year-old doll and she treats my friends and me to an expensive day out. BEST. NEIGHBOR. EVER.

Dad parks in the section of the garage designated for vehicles with handicapped plates. Turns out my dad called the Guest Services Department at the Staples Center last week so our seats are accessible for Umberto's wheelchair.

designated

The afternoon is AMAZING— screaming, chanting, and eating followed by more screaming, chanting, and eating. (Hot dogs, chili, tacos, soda, chips, and ice cream were involved.) My dad even

souvenir

bought each of us Monster Truck souvenir hats.

"I'm not sure if this is better than the moon bouncer," Matt says through a mouthful of popcorn.

"I actually had fun that day," Carly answers.

You've got to love that girl's optimism.

"All I know is, we're getting on the Jumbotron," Umberto says. "I don't care what we have to do."

We spend the next round of Monster Truck action waving our arms in the air, trying to catch the attention of the many cameras in the Staples Center. Matt goes so far as to limbo up the aisle but there's so much activity going on around us that even the nearby spectators barely pay attention.

spectators

It's a great afternoon that I don't want to end but during the last Monster Truck demonstration, my dad starts gathering up his things. I thank him for a great day.

"It was all Mrs. Mitchell," he says.

When I turn back to my friends, Umberto is tossing French fries into Matt's mouth while Carly looks on, shaking her head at our immaturity. I grab some fries from Umberto's tray and stick one into each of my ears.

"You look like a Martian with potato antennae," Matt says.

I gaze at the two thick French fries still in my hand, then shove one up each nostril.

nostril

All three of my friends let out a giant "Ewwwwwww!" while my

Frankenstein

father gives me his Stop-That-Now face.

But instead, I walk between our seats like Frankenstein until Umberto starts screaming again. "Look!"

I follow his gaze to the Jumbotron that now shows a giant video of me with the caption FRENCH FRY BOY.

Laughter ripples throughout the auditorium; even my father can't keep a straight face. I feel myself flush with embarrassment—are people laughing with me or AT me? I look at the video one more time. It IS kind of funny. If it were some other kid in a different section of the Staples Center, I'd be laughing too. I feel myself begin to smile, then turn to Matt.

I look at him.

He looks at me.

"Do it," Matt says. "I dare you."

And before Carly can reach for my hand to stop me, I stare into the camera and grab the fries from my ears and nose and feed them one by one into my mouth. The crowd erupts in laughter and groans; the caption now reads GROSS! in giant letters.

"You really ARE a joke," Umberto says.

"An awesome one," Matt agrees.

Carly shakes her head. "At least you're consistent."

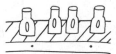

consistent

I watch the instant replay on the video and figure the rest of this year might still end up okay, even if I'm not the tower of maturity I thought I'd be when it started. As I bow to the crowd's applause, I wonder if learning to laugh at yourself for doing something wrong or stupid might even be a step in the right direction. I reach for another French fry.

"Don't even think about it," my father says.

So much for a standing ovation.

ovation

Here's a sneak peek at
the first chapter of

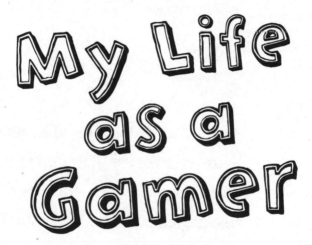

coming soon!

An Offer I Can't Refuse

castaway

Here's the thing no one tells you about monkeys: They steal your cereal every chance they get. Lucky Charms, Cocoa Puffs, Froot Loops, Trix, Gorilla Munch—even the boring ones like Grape Nuts—drive my capuchin monkey, Frank, out of his mind. He's like a castaway who finally gets to dry land and can't wait to eat everything in sight. I hate keeping him locked in his cage like a prisoner while I eat in front of him every morning. But on the days I let him out, the kitchen ends up looking like a rainbow war zone with flakes and nuggets all over the floor. My mutt, Bodi, is much more well behaved, waiting patiently for me to measure out his food and place it in the bowl near the bookcase.

nuggets

measure

"How about some chocolate chip pancakes?" my dad asks.

I say yes, mainly so I can take Frank out of his cage. (Frank is not a fan of pancakes.)

My dad's been out of work for the last two months, so he's on kitchen patrol. He's been a freelance storyboard artist since before I was born, but the industry's in a slump and it's been hard for him to find new work. Luckily, my mom is a veterinarian, so they've still been able to pay the bills. The good news is that my father's been experimenting with lots of great new recipes. The bad news is that he's taken an even greater interest in my homework.

experimenting

Since I was little, the best way for me to learn my vocabulary words was to draw them. I have notebooks and notebooks and notebooks filled with illustrations of stick figures acting out my words. My parents have always inspected my work, but now Dad is putting each drawing under a microscope.

inspected

"Are you sure that's the best definition of *inquire*?" he asks, scanning my notebook.

microscope

"Shouldn't we add more chocolate chips to the batter?" I ask, changing the subject.

"When I worked on that last film at Sony, they wanted every detail just right." My dad throws another handful of chips into the bowl. "Every line, every letter had to be exact."

Now I wish I'd just had cereal. I'd rather be sweeping up Cap'n Crunch than listening to Dad reflective about his work. I hope he gets a new job soon—I'll miss the pancakes, but not the sad stories.

reflective

"Hey, I forgot to tell you," Dad says. "I got an e-mail from one of the Sony guys yesterday to see if I knew any kids who might be interested in testing some new software." He gently places three pancakes on my plate.

"Sony!" I shout. "Was he talking about testing video games?"

My dad pours himself a second

cup of coffee. "Does that mean you're interested?"

I don't even bother with maple syrup. I roll the three pancakes into a log, yell good-bye to my dad, Bodi, and Frank, then race to school to share the news with my friends.

WE'RE GOING TO GET PAID TO TEST VIDEO GAMES!

About the Author

Janet Tashjian is the author of many popular novels, including *My Life as a Book*, *My Life as a Stuntboy*, *My Life as a Cartoonist*, and her new series, Einstein the Class Hamster. Other books include *The Gospel According to Larry*, *Vote for Larry*, and *Larry and the Meaning of Life* as well as *Fault Line*, *For What It's Worth*, *Multiple Choice*, *Tru Confessions*, and *Marty Frye, Private Eye*. She lives with her family in Los Angeles.
www.janettashjian.com

author

About the Illustrator

Jake Tashjian is the illustrator of *My Life as a Book*, *My Life as a Stuntboy*, *My Life as a Cartoonist*, and the new series, Einstein the Class Hamster. He has been drawing pictures of his vocabulary words on index cards since he was a kid and now has a stack taller than a house. When he's not drawing, he loves to surf, read comic books, and watch movies.

illustrator